FORGED
BLADE

NASH BLACK

Other books by Nash Black

Novels

Ono County Series
Book 1 - *Prelude of Death*
Book 2 - *Cards of Death*

Young Brothers Series
Book 1 - *Sandprints of Death*
Book 2 - *Catspaw of Death*

Capital Crimes Series
Book 1 - *Forged Blade*

Ono County Ghostly Tales
Haints
Games of Death

Non-Fiction

Writing as a Small Business

An Evan Blade Detective Novel

FORGED BLADE

NASH BLACK

Capital Crime Series, Volume 1

Jamestown, Kentucky

© Copyright 2017, IF Publishing Company

First published in this edition 2017

IF Publishing Company, Jamestown, KY

ISBN: 978-0-9839941-6-9

The cover for *Forged Blade* was created by Stuart Simpson.

Interior design: Dean Fetzer, GunBoss Books,
www.gunboss.com

This is a work of fiction. Names, characters, places, and incidents either are the product of the author's imagination or are used fictitiously, and any resemblance to persons living or dead is entirely coincidental.

Dedication

To the *Fruit of the Lens Camera Club* of Somerset Community College, Somerset, KY, who named their annual Earth Day monetary awards for us. The Nash Black Photography Award is an honor we cherish. Thank you for your friendship and support through the years.

Characters

Evan Blade – detective

Petra Isolta "Pi" McIntyre

Charity Sims – housekeeper, Hawaiian mix

Desper Sims – Charity's husband

Clayton Forrester – Pi's guardian

Curtis Burton Colton – Lieutenant State Police

Madeline "Maddy" Sorals – cleaning service

Jordan Ames – Ono County lawyer & Marcus McIntyre's stepson

Wedge and Anvil Forge – Evan Blade's assistants

Innis Morgan – Pi's biological father

Thornton Thomas Towbridge – Lieutenant Governor

Chapter 1

Blood.

Blood drips from the kid's hand.

I round the kitchen island in two strides. Clayton Forrester lies on the floor clutching a towel to his middle. His eyes focus on me then close.

"I'll hold on. Hide her before ambulance…envelope. Call Maddy…knows what to do. Car in drive…garage. Keep her safe. Cops'll get wind."

Scramble to my feet. Clayton said, 'her.' A girl?

Kid's so sexless she wouldn't attract a blind drunk in a dark bar. Can't be more than twelve or so. Not tall enough.

Stares into space from blank honey colored eyes.

Wave my hand in her face. Doesn't blink. Unseeing. Hasn't moved from where I shoved her to get to Clayton.

She's holding two brown packets against an old double breasted pea coat.

Yank paper towels from the roller. Give them a swipe under the spigot to clean the blood from her hand so it won't drip on me.

Kid doesn't move. Tan eyes flecked with green wide open. It's like cleaning a statue.

"Little…doesn't remember. Hide her." Clayton rasps from the floor.

Scoop her up and run down the hall. She curls into me like a small kitten. Dump her on a sofa in front room. Run back to the kitchen to call Maddy.

"Found Clayton. He's alive. Conscious. Leaking like a busted hose."

"Where?"

"McIntyre's kitchen."

"Help is on the way. Clean up the mess."

"Maddy, I'm not one of your maids. It's going on one AM."

"Get busy. Park your truck out of sight. Stop stalling." She cuts the connection.

Running back to the house through an alley as the ambulance pulls up to the gate from the opposite direction. Open it to let them pass. Latch it against the garage so they won't waste time getting out.

Two guys have Clayton wrapped, rolled on a gurney with an IV drip in less than five minutes. They ignore me as if I'm invisible.

Thank God, Maddy sent a private service. They don't ask questions I can't answer. Closing the back door when the phone rings.

"Are they gone?"

"Out the gate. He's breathing."

"He'll make it. Not the first time."

"Where are they taking him?"

"Private clinic. Have a surgeon waiting who owes me."

"Did he tell you anything?"

"Take care of the kid and hide her car."

"She is there! Did anyone see her?"

"No. Out cold. Looks like shock. Found Clayton first. Stashed her in the front parlor."

"Clean up evidence. Move her car, put it in the back garage. Clayton has a pad above it. Sack out there until Desper and Charity Sims arrive. Everything must look normal."

Take a quick look at the kid. Still out. There's one of those handmade yarn things and an old stuffed elephant in the hall by a knapsack. She barely moves when I remove the pea coat, wrap her in the cover and place the elephant beside her. Her arm clasps it to her chest.

Breathing even. In a deep sleep. She's okay. Kids went comatose from seeing blood in 'Nam.

On my way back to the kitchen, I hang the old coat in a closet. Who needs a heavy coat in June?

~ ~ ~

Whoof follows me up the stairs inside the garage to Clayton's bolt-hole. Use my flashlight to look around.

Not bad. Army barracks sparse. Comfortable cot and small chest, easy chair with floor lamp, john with shower, unit type kitchen, and dark green roller shades over the windows. Turn on the lamp and toss the place.

Fishing rods and gear are hanging on one wall. Few clothes in a tiny closet, stack of books by chair, and a short wave radio tuned to police channel. Find his empty gun safe behind a kitchen cabinet.

Pull a Falls City from the little fridge and sink into the chair. Whoof stakes out the small rug by the bed and watches me. Only dog I've ever had who can doze with one eye open.

Sleep's impossible until I sort the evening's events in my mind. When I open a new case I use a mental diary support by rough notes of every detail until I get a chance to type it out on my old Royal.

Maddy called around ten-thirty. Run our conversation through the gears.

"Get your ass out of bed. Find him."

"Find who?"

"Clayton, you miserable carney turd."

"Didn't know he was lost."

"Don't have time for your dumb ass remarks. He has been shot."

"Shot? As in dead?"

"Evan Blade, we can't find a body. Pack your best bib-and-tucker. Got to look respectable. Bring the twins, the kid arrives this afternoon."

"Why can no one can locate him? What kid?"

"Don't know. My source was gigging along the river and saw it. Described him to a 'T.' By the time he climbed the bank Clayton was gone.

"He called me. Didn't want to get hauled in on a drunk charge if he reported a murder with no body."

"Slow down."

"Go to back door. Someone is in the house. Lights are on in the kitchen. My guy saw shadows move across a window."

"What house?"

"Marcus McIntyre's at 1453 Clay Avenue. Go in from the alley so noisy neighbors won't see you.

"Find Clayton. He has a efficiency above the garage."

"If he's alive, then he's hid. Check bushes."

"Will do. Get up here pronto.

"Don't pick up any speeding tickets. My fixer's nose is out-of-joint about the last time."

Grab worn clothes, which are okay for the drive to Capital City. Dig around in the back of a closet for a garment bag, pack, and donned my.38 for easy access.

Called Anvil Forge to tell him to stand by for trouble. His wife, Doris took Bobbi Vance, my foster daughter to the movies. She's spending the night with them rather than come down the steep path to my houseboat in the dark. Told him not to wake her.

No need for Anvil or his brother, Wedge on the scene to bust heads until I know what's going down.

Whoof danced at my heels, anticipating a late night run. Include dog food in the bag.

Maddy Sorals wasn't prone to hysterics. Been around the block too many times.

Her news sources are questionable. Deadly accurate. She supplements her Social Security operating a cleaning service of professional snoops. Moonlights as my secretary because she had a soft spot for my foster grandfather, Aloysius Thornton.

First time I saw Clayton Forrester, he sauntered across the border from Cambodia into 'Nam, as if he was out for a Sunday afternoon stroll, using what was left of his shirt for a sling. Eating a melting Hershey bar.

We were hunkered down waiting for med-a-vac to lift us out of a snake pit. Lieutenant had taken off with the rest of our outfit to clean out a nest of vipers so the chopper would have clear landing space.

Stepped on a pongee stake and cut an artery in my foot. Abel Young was afraid I'd bleed to death before the Huey arrived. His tourniquet wasn't helping much. Got light headed. Abel had six other grunts worse off than me to keep alive. Clayton ordered him to tend to them while he took care of the hopping wounded.

He was a civilian who'd seen some hurt. Long jagged scar ran down from behind his left ear to under the sling. Old scar from another war.

He pulled the artery from my foot. Held his good thumb on it. Releasing it at intervals all the way to the triage station after he'd flashed some kind of identification to the pilot who questioned his climbing on board.

Gunner took a hit. He took over the machine gun and proved he knew how to use it without creasing the starch in his pants.

Abel was out of morphine so Clayton used twelve year old malt he had in a flask to swab out my foot. We drank the rest and arrived drunker than raw recruits on their first liberty. He saved my foot and possibly my life.

In the recovery tent, we got to talking to avoid screaming and discovered we were both from Ono County when I told him about Lieutenant Curtis Burton Colton's recruitment procedures. He started laughing when he recognized the string of names.

Curt put together a hell of an outfit, using a midnight raid on personnel records and a glib tongue: Abel Young, a camera toting medic from Clydesville, and the twins, Wedge and Anvil Forge from Ovendecker Bottom. He was determined to go home standing up and take us with him.

Weird how things turn out. Curt's still a lieutenant for the State Police. Abel got himself appointed sheriff of Allerton County. It wasn't until later we learned Abel also has a twin. Wedge and Anvil are my backup when things get rougher than my 185 pounds can handle.

Me. Made myself a private investigator after a bad patch on an out-of-state police force. Kentucky doesn't pay attention to private detectives. Covers the overhead and provides eating money. Doubtful if when averaged it pays better than a minimum wage job, but I call the shots.

Curt wouldn't hire me because he said my fingers were too nimble after my extensive schooling in the sawdust of the carnival circuit.

Clayton Forrester drifts in and out of lives like a ghost. Don't know what kind of ID he carried that allowed him a 'no-questions-asked' ride out of the jungle. Glad he was around.

Promised him I'd look after the kid. She can join Bobbi at the lake, where no one can find her until Clayton can get back on the job. He's never mentioned having a ward.

Closed mouthed about his life. Understands why I work to stay in the background. A few thugs out there who have a vested interest in putting an end to my breathing.

Owe him. I will find out who plugged him and left me saddled with a brat.

Chapter 2

I'm tired and hungry.

Matron would tell me I'm dithering.

The house I came so far to find is on the corner of a quite street above a river. It fronts against a herringbone inlaid brick walk. A long brick wall with a gate is joined to the house. I park beside it and walk to the entrance. A double stair leads up three steps to the front door much like the old houses in Philadelphia.

I'm afraid to punch the ivory doorbell I've driven from Annapolis to locate. Afraid of what lies beyond the portal.

A sliver of light from the cloud crossed moon strikes a highly polished brass plate above the button.

P.I. McIntyre.

A name engraved on the plate. The initials are the same as mine for, Petra Isolta McIntyre. Reads like a detective in a old novel. Some detective I'll make since I've never discovered who I am, but it looks discreet and dignified.

I jam the bell. Hear a muffled jangle in the distance. No one comes to answer my summons. Impatiently I wait, then punch the button a second and third time. I know it's late and I'm a day early. I didn't want to stop overnight in a motel.

Didn't estimate correctly how long it would take to get to Capital City, Kentucky from Annapolis, Maryland, in my Metropolitan. The big trucks almost blew me off the road when they roared past.

George Stanopolis wouldn't let me take his baby out alone until he was sure I could handle her in any situation, on and off the road. A vision of him folded up and overflowing the passenger seat makes me smile in spite of my exhaustion.

The house is dark – maybe everyone is asleep though there are lights in the house across the street.

A gust of wind carrying the scent of honeysuckle darts around the corner of the house cutting though my clothes as if I'm naked in a fierce gale off the sound.

Running back to my car to get my jacket I remember the set of keys Mrs. Strove handed me when I left the coast to come to Capital City. Clayton Forrester had left them with her for safe keeping until I needed them.

Shrug into my old pea coat I'd stuffed behind the seat. It was too big to pack with my other clothes.

I dig the set of keys out of the knapsack, sling it over my shoulder. Then grab my night case, throw Strovie's afghan over my arm, and stuff Dumbo on top. Before I close the door I pull out my walking stick and put it under my arm.

It's a lazy man's load. I don't want to have to make another trip outside tonight. The rest can wait until morning.

After two tries, the third key slides into the lock and the door glides open on well oiled hinges into a vestibule lit by the street light on the corner. A second set of doors, with intricate panes of stained glass set in lead strips and another lock confronts me. A hall tree stands on one side waiting for guests to shed their coats. I'm too cold to use it.

I fumble with the keys until I find the one to fit the second lock. The tinkle of a small bell over my head announces my entrance into a spacious hallway, with double doors on both sides, single doors beyond them and one at the back. All closed and forbidding, as if the house has been shut up for a long time.

As I step over the threshold soft lights glow from wall sconces placed at intervals down the hall. I expect a staircase leading to the second floor. There isn't one.

I pull the door closed behind me and hear the gentle click of the lock. The house feels abandoned, frozen in time. A musky odor of void floats around me as if my presence has stirred something old and best forgotten.

The reddish-brown of the walls below a walnut chair rail are carved leather. I run my fingers over the embossed leaves and vines. Soft and well cared for, a masculine surface. A heavy cream silk fabric of the same pattern is stretched to the ceiling above the rail. The hall has a aura of a male domain and age like it has been this way since the house was built.

My fingers itch to open a window to admit the wind to blow the past from the hall. Instead I dump my stuff by a small table beside the oak double doors, messing up the pristine elegance of the hall.

The doors don't have knobs. Instead there are finger spaces to push them back into the wall. The ones on the right open into a large library. Heavy curtains cover the windows facing the street. I grope for a light switch. A large fireplace, surrounded by a green veined marble mantle occupies the far wall, with loaded book shelves extending down to each corner of the square room.

The room is similar to the main reading room at St. Johns where I went to college.

A metallic odor overrides a faint smell of lemony furniture polish, unlike the hallway. This room definitely needs fresh air. It's immaculate, except for the huge walnut desk and tables. Every plane is covered with folders and scattered papers, as if the owner was suddenly called away.

I've intruded into a private domain. I retreat and pull the heavy doors closed on the deadly silence.

Across the hall are the same doors. I open them, find the light switch. A duplicate of the one behind me, except it is arranged as parlor or reception room, with great cabbage roses tossed at random on the walls against a black background. A wild room. The huge flowers appear to move, making my head spin.

Leave the doors open to spread light into the hall.

Driven by the unseen force of curiosity I make my way to the next set of doors. The first opens to an empty closet that smells like a cedar forest. The other is a utilitarian powder room, a much needed facility.

Beyond the back door is a large kitchen with every imaginable appliance.

I gasp, "You could feed the cadets from here," before I realize I'm talking to myself though my stomach agrees with me.

I find a tea kettle, fill it with water and set it on the range to boil then rummage through the cabinets until I locate a box of tea bags. The refrigerator is well stocked with provisions for breakfast and sandwiches. I pile thin slices of ham and cheese on bread slathered with a spicy mustard, while my tea brews.

After a few bites, I slow down to eat like a civilized person. I'm eating to hide my loneliness. A tan envelope lies on the corner of the island. I pull it towards me. My name is on it, so I'm not snooping in someone else's business when I open it.

Inside is an estate deed of conveyance for the house wrapped around a packet of one hundred dollar bills. The deed is made out to me with my name fully spelled out from the estate of Marcus Laurence McIntyre. It had been executed by an Elton Laurence Fightmaster, fifteen years ago.

According to the deed, I own this house and grounds located at 1453 Clay Avenue, Capital City, Kentucky. The wording is a simple verbal description of the boundaries mentioning the brick wall and a garage opening to an alley. There isn't any mention of who owned the house prior to Marcus McIntyre. The house, from the little I've seen, has been well maintained.

A home…a place of my own. This house was deeded to me, soon after I arrived at the Valley View Children's Home. My first clear memory.

I have owned this house since I was five years old.

~ ~ ~

Tears. I can't stop them.

I'm howling like I did when I fell down the stairs and broke my leg. Matron isn't here to slap my face and promise to give me something to cry about if I didn't stop acting like a baby.

The silence of the house drowns the unk unk of my hiccups.

I drop my half-eaten sandwich back on the plate and slide off the high stool. Hold my nose and count to ten. My heart is thumping in my ears as the tears cease.

I'm shaking with cold as if I'll never get warm again.

I catch my reflection in the window of the kitchen alcove. I'm slumped over the island beating my fist against the hard surface. There is no one to see how stupid I'm behaving.

No one, but me.

I pitch the unfinished sandwich in the garbage can beneath the sink, take a gulp of the tepid tea (gone tannic) and rush back down the hall to the lavatory.

Mrs. Strove, my landlady in Maryland, is the one person I've known as a friend. She is blind. She has never seen me, though she recognized the well of loneliness I sealed in and she rescued me from despair. I pull her wisdom around me like the constant movement of the ocean and return to the kitchen.

I'm still freezing – though it's June. I can't get warm. My pea coat is on the floor, by the range where I'd dropped it, while making tea. I shrug into it.

I'd cleaned the island of my half-eaten meal before I went to the bathroom to make repairs. Now there is a marble rolling pin lying across a second brown envelope beside the deed.

I move the heavy pin. Again my name appears, I pick it up wondering what additional shocks await me. Hidden beneath it is a scrawled note.

No help for it. Stay in the house.

Dangerous. Evan will call. Safe with him.

A messy signature staggers down the page.

Clayton.

Clayton Forrester was my guardian until I became twenty-one on my birthday in February. I haven't heard one word from him since he sent me a dozen yellow roses with a note saying he was proud of me.

He didn't come to my graduation. Mrs. Strove and her next door neighbor, Micki Stiles were my surrogate family at the ceremony.

I pick up the second brown envelope and turn it over to unfold the brass fastenings. Red spots are scattered on the back side.

My elbow hits the rolling pin. It rolls over, revealing the upside down print of a man's hand.

Rusty colored like drying blood.

I inch around the island terrified at what I'll find.

A man with wolf eyes is lying on the floor. He reaches for my hand.

The room spins as the backdoor opens.

Chapter 3

"Miss McIntyre."

I jerk awake, confused as to where I am and tumble to the floor. A thousand thorns are prickling my skin from where I've slept too hard. Kick, to extract my legs from the twisted afghan.

"I'm in the parlor."

Crawl up on my knees and look over the back of the davenport at a tall woman wearing a brightly colored mu-mu and leather sandals.

"Mother Mary! Mr. Forrester said you'd arrive this afternoon. We've left you here with no food in the house."

While she is talking, she helps me to my feet then picks up the afghan, folds it, pats the crushed cushion into shape, and places Dumbo beside it.

I hold out my hand, "I'm Petra McIntyre, but everyone calls me, 'Pi' like in circumference. You are?"

"Charity Sims. My Desper and I take care of your place for Mr. Forrester. He keeps an apartment over the garage. The electricity will be back on in a jiffy. I saw the men working on the transformer as we drove in. Lightening must have struck it during the storm. The very idea…leaving you stranded in this big house in the dark.

"Let me have your keys and Desper will bring in your things."

"Sure, I could use some help. It's out front by the white gate…"

"No, it isn't. It's in the garage. I saw it through the window. Cute convertible, just your size. What is it?"

"A Nash Metropolitan."

Strange, I left my car out front. I know I did.

"I'm from the islands. I made that man marry me before he went off to warring. I wasn't going to be left with a souvenir like my mama, to be reared by the Sisters. They were good, saintly women who could make a child feel lower than low because no one wanted them. Like being abandoned on the church doorstep was their fault."

"I know." I mutter as she pauses for a breath.

"There are scrubs at the yard from Hawaii."

"Scrubs?"

"Excuse me, cadets at the Navel Academy in Annapolis where I went to school."

"You're in the Navy?"

"No, no, I went to St. Johns College. Both are in the same town in Maryland."

I feel a kinship with this golden statuesque woman. Her

ebony hair is pulled into a thick coil on her neck laced with fire-shot ribbons.

She pulls open the drapes and gives them a shake. Little flakes of dust dance in the beams of sunlight. The ominous strain of the house evaporates before Charity's exuberant personality.

"Come in the kitchen and keep me company while I grind coffee beans. I'll have them ready to perk when the power is restored."

She pauses by the right-hand doors and pulls them apart.

"Look at this mess. I cleaned it for you. Now look at it. Phew, smells too."

She quickly pulls the doors closed.

"We'll leave the drapes shut. Don't want your neighbors thinking I don't know how to take proper care of you."

"Charity, I need to freshen up."

I pick up my overnight case and hand her my keys I'd left on the table, beside the items I carried in last night.

Weird. The afghan and Dumbo were on the floor with my knapsack and train case. I dropped them before I looked in the rooms and discovered the kitchen.

"Right in there."

She points to the powder room.

"We'll check around upstairs after I fix you some breakfast to see which room suits you."

~ ~ ~

19

My hair is twisted in knots of curls standing on end and my eyes resemble a hazard map of Chesapeake Bay. I hold a washcloth soaked in cold water against my face, scrub my teeth, and pull a brush through the tangles.

Medusa the Terrible isn't the way to meet new people. It will have to do until I can find a place to shower and change my travel stained clothes.

Curley brown hair, faint freckles on a summer tanned skin. Shadowed, dusty-brown eyes a friend was kind enough to describe as devil woman's, stare back at me from the mirror. I look the same as I did in the eighth grade when I discovered a mirror for the first time in the big girls' bathroom.

I've never grown up.

My face won't launch ships or be the one to whom poets write sonnets, but maybe it will get me through breakfast with the exotic Charity.

The earthy aroma of coffee beans tickles my nose as I enter the kitchen. Charity is tossing them in a frying pan over a high flame, mixing and stirring so fast the bracelets on her arm jingle.

A ping sounds from the microwave, the lights flicker and then blaze. I'd turned on every light in the kitchen last night. I walk around turning them off as Charity pours the roasted beans in a grinder. The smell is so strong my stomach aches for a cup of coffee, though I normally drink tea.

She glances out the window.

"Desper is at the back door. Please, hold it open for him while I get the coffee started."

A dark man is pulling a cart up the steps. He is taller and broader than Charity. Muscles in his powerful arms move as he tugs the load into the kitchen.

"Books are heavy. Do you want to put these in the library?"

His soft voice is a surprise coming from so large a body. I haven't had time to think where I want my books. For that matter, do I want to stay in this strange house I know nothing about?

Where can I go?

Clayton instructed me to come here and left me the deed.

Before I answer, Charity says, "Leave them inside the library door. Mr. Forrester left a mess in there."

He grins and winks at me behind her back.

"Yes, woman, I know. Smells good in here."

He continues to walk backwards and uses his shoulder to open the swinging door to the hall.

Chapter 4

"Charity. Call the police. Mr. Dialman is down behind the desk."

"What...?"

"Don't waste time asking fool questions I can't answer."

I start toward the door. He shakes his head.

"Please, Miss McIntyre, stay in the kitchen. You're not supposed to be here. Nothing we can do for him."

Charity dials the phone.

"Desper was in the army. He knows trouble."

She talks to the dispatcher, asking for help at 1453 Clay Avenue.

A wave of nausea hits me. The copper odor, when I opened the doors to the library last night, was blood.

Charity darts to the counter and dumps a heaping tablespoon of sugar into a cup. She pours the half-brewed coffee over it and shoves it across the island toward me.

"Drink. You can get nervy later."

"Who...is...Mr. Dialman?"

"Lives across the street. Kind of looks after your place when we're not here."

I drink the coffee. Sickeningly sweet doesn't hide the foul taste of bitter medicine.

Why is a neighbor dead in my library? The possessive pronoun startles me.

Billy Bejaysus. This is my house.

A bit ago I was thinking about leaving. I'm tired of not having a home. I'm standing my ground. Keeping what's mine no matter how many bodies turn up.

Charity whirls and races through the door.

I peek. She goes in the parlor. Comes out carrying my things, which she puts in the closet. I catch her eye and point to the bathroom. She catches my meaning. Gets the traincase and the wet washcloth and towel.

"Mother Mary! I almost forgot."

She runs back down the hall into the library and pulls out the cart with my books and shoves them in the closet.

She thumbs through the phone book, makes a call and says one word, "Trouble" before she hangs up. Then dials a second time from memory.

"Maddy, Dialman is in the library. Dead."

"Don't know."

"Here with me."

She listens, her face goes pale as she gulps for air. Then it goes cold and blank.

"I see. Okay, will do."

We both jump when a siren blares at the front of the house. She rushes back down the hall. I hold the door open enough to watch.

She closes the parlor doors, looks in the library, nods her head and goes to the front door. A burley policeman is standing in the vestibule. She points to the library and doesn't say a word. She moves in front of the parlor doors, out of the way with her eyes glued to the open doors across the hall.

I start out of the kitchen. Her hand motions me to stay where I am. The policeman comes out of the library, nods to her, and goes out the front door, leaving it open.

Charity closes it and enters the library. The front bell rings, she closes the doors before she answers the urgent summons.

Two policemen are standing on the threshold with Desper between them. She backs into the hall.

"Is this guy your husband?" A hard rough voice asks.

"Yes. We take care of the house for Mr. Forrester."

Charity makes no move to invite the men in though Mr. Dialman's body is in the library. She stands as stiff as a flagpole facing them.

"Show me where the stiff was shot."

Desper looks at the man holding his arm and gently removes his hand.

"I don't know where he was shot. It wasn't in this house."

"Darkie, how would you know?" Hard voice yells at him.

"Officer, I spent three years in Korea as a medic. There aren't any blood splatters in the room and as you said he is stiff."

He pulls open the library doors.

"See for yourself."

They enter and stay for what seems like hours.

"Don't you go getting lost. We'll have more to discuss when my people get here." Hard voice says as they come back into the hall.

"I've lived in Capital City all my life, don't plan on going anywhere. Now, may my wife make coffee?"

"Sure. Could use some. You listen. You may talk fancy and have a high-yellow Chink for a wife, but it doesn't cut any ice with the department."

"My mother taught English at Ed Davis High School and my father was the principal. He also coached football."

Hard voice stomps up close, peers into his face. His voice changes to awe, "Desper Joe Sims. You broke my nose."

"You deserved it for un-sportsmanship conduct when you kneed me in the groin, Billy Ray Johnson."

Officer Johnson sticks out his hand. Desper responds. They both are laughing at something I can't hear as Charity opens the front door for them. I'll swear her hands flutter in a shooing motion.

I shake my head. Men have no sense when it comes to sports.

~ ~ ~

Charity gets mugs which don't match, out of a cabinet and loads them on a tray. I fill them while she fixes a jug of milk and bowl of sugar. After making the delivery she comes back to the kitchen, empties the last of the coffee beans in a skillet, banging it up and down while explaining to me what is happening.

Hours pass as we sit sipping tea. I'd made some for myself while she was serving the men their coffee. She is reusing the grounds with a little fresh added to the pot. I can't help grinning as I watch her eke out the supply.

Finally, Desper returns to tell us they've gone across the street to check Mr. Dialman's house, as it's obvious his body had been hidden in the library, after being shot somewhere else.

Desper tells us Mr. Dialman had been beaten with what he thinks was a rubber garden hose before he was shot. Then explains the state police crime lab should be able to pin point the identity of the instrument when they perform the autopsy.

They found a side window-door, opening into the walled garden, unlatched and assumed this was the point of entry.

Desper had the misfortune to find the body when he took my books to the library.

For now, it's off limits until the police can search for fingerprints and finish their investigation. Mine would be on the door pulls and the light switch. I didn't touch anything else in the room. Charity and Desper's fingerprints should cover mine since they both opened the door and turned on the light after I did.

He leaves to mow the lawn and to appear unconcerned if anyone is watching.

She tells me Mr. Forrester has been detained by a personal emergency. He has left strict orders I'm not to be seen or leave the house until he talks to me.

I resent this. He is no longer officially my guardian.

It's June. According to my fake hospital birth certificate I was twenty-two on February fourteenth. My investigating lead me to Blackwell, Virginia. Thelma Burton Curtis, listed as my mother, was an old woman buried five years before I was born. The Bureau of Vital Statistics had no record of a Brenda Curtis Burton, born a year before my supposed birth date. The ghost man no longer has the power to park me in obscure places like a pawn on a chess board.

Charity cuts the center out of two slices of homemade bread and fries them on one side. She flips the toast and drops eggs in the holes. Then covers the skillet with a glass lid while bacon sizzles in another skillet.

"Who were you talking to on the phone?"

"Madeline Sorals, she's Mr. Forrester's secretary. I was worried. He promised us he'd be here when you arrived."

"His problems must be serious. Your face went white when you were talking to her."

"They are."

"I meant the first phone call when you said, 'trouble' and hung up."

"It was his answering service. He instructed us to report any trouble to that number and then call Mrs. Sorals."

The eggs, when she slides the toast on a plate are done to perfection. I'm ashamed of myself as to how I devour her simple meal. In one respect it's a production to cater to a child. An attempt on her part to distract me from the events of the morning.

A wasted effort to keep me from voicing the incessant questions rampaging through my mind. I'm positive she doesn't have the answers.

"Delicious. I was starving. Join me for another cup of tea."

"Last one. Someone made tea last night and dumped a half-eaten ham sandwich in the garbage. Attracts ants."

"Oh, I did it. I'm sorry. Didn't think."

"Don't worry. I fed it to a big German Shepard who wandered in from the alley.

"There isn't enough food in this house to feed a half-grown pup. I keep sandwich things in the refrigerator to fix Desper a spot of lunch when he does up the yard. I meant to go shopping this morning.

"We didn't expect you until this afternoon."

"Don't change your plans because of me. Go to the grocery."

"You'll be here alone. Mr. Clayton won't like it."

"Charity, we have an emergency situation. I'll lock all the doors when you leave. Who knows I'm here since Desper parked my car in the garage?"

"He didn't touch it. It was there when we arrived."

"Someone…someone who could walk, was in the house last night."

A shudder runs down my spine, but I can't let her see I'm scared. I fake Matron's take-charge voice to calm my fears. It puts a stop to my dithering.

"I've been alone as far back as I can remember. I will be careful. When you get back, you can tell me about Mr. Forrester. He may have been my guardian, but I've seldom laid eyes on the man. I have a lot of questions he must answer before I can live here."

"What do you mean? This is your home."

"It isn't often a neighbor's body is found in one's library on their first day in residence."

My foray into sarcasm gains me a reluctant grin.

Our eyes lock in common recognition. We'd both been home schooled and survived.

"Does Mr. Forrester know you have fangs?"

Chapter 5

"Stuck in Clayton's pad until the cops clear out. Desper told me what went down in the house. Dialman lived across the street. What was he doing in McIntyre's house?"

"My source said he was dead or almost when he was dumped. Did you go in the library last night?"

"No. No reason to."

"Good, you're getting smarter. Wait a sec."

Maddy keeps the phone company in business. She has four phones on separate lines. I'm one of the privileged who knows all of her numbers.

"Back. Guy from hospital. He says Dialman has been dead over 12, but under 20 hours. Hard to pin down. They will know more when they do the autopsy."

"I've got to finish some work for Towbridge I left hanging. The twins can keep an eye on the kid."

"Towbridge keeps you around to do his dirty work."

"Pays the bills."

"Evan. Towbridge can wait. He uses the information you dig up to keep his adversaries in line so they don't forget he is a power. Clayton is depending on us to keep the kid safe from predators."

"Why is she a target?"

"Simple. Bonehead. Clayton has spent fifteen years building a wall around her. Moving her to places no one has ever heard of like an obscure Catholic boarding school and the egghead college she attended in Maryland.

"He found her beside McIntyre's body."

"Ancient history."

"True as far as it goes. McIntyre's killer may have known she was there. Now someone has tried to kill Clayton. The kid is the key. The killer may believe she can point the finger at him."

"Okay, I see. What's the word from the hospital?"

"Private clinic. Alive and out of surgery. It's going to be touch and go. He'd almost bled out by the time you arrived. Where is Desper?"

"Mowing the lawn and keeping an eye pealed while Charity gets groceries. Glad the boys in blue can't see over the wall. He's been at it over an hour on a postage stamp. Trying to wipe out the tracks of the ambulance. The kid's in the living quarters unpacking."

"Call her and take her out to lunch."

"What? She doesn't know me."

"Tell her Clayton sent you since he couldn't come himself."

Clayton will make it. He didn't want to go to a hospital where a person could die.

He did a messy, but adequate job packing his wound with towels. Knows how to treat himself. He was almost blown apart at Kumsong in Korea yet managed to stay alive by stuffing his wounds with dead men's clothes until some Turks found him.

Never said what he does to earn a paycheck. He has pulled more than one set of balls out of the fire. Good man to know and not one to be taken unawares. Knows who shot him.

Call the twins and give them their orders. They'll be bunking at Clayton's place with strict orders not to go anywhere together. This will be hard on Wedge and Anvil as they only have one brain between them. They're dead ass loyal. Clayton Forrester is their idol on the right hand of Lieutenant Colton.

I follow orders. Surprised when the kid agrees. Desper gives me the all clear. Take off to clean up. Two hours to kill.

Chapter 6

Charity showed me the door to the residence side of the house. Strange, it's inside a pantry-laundry room. The instant I stepped through the door to the main hall I know what little memory I have isn't wrong.

The library and reception rooms had been partitioned from the family residence. The hall is broader with a curved staircase along one wall. The same cool marble floor. Black and white diamonds parade toward the front door. My adult feet are planted squarely in the middle so I won't step on a crack. It invites bad luck.

I open the front door. It's different, just one inlaid with colored glass, then a regular storm door opening out onto a porch the length of the house.

Walk to the corner and study the structure. Two smaller houses have been joined. There is a faint difference in the color of the bricks where they connect.

When I glance across the street to where a half-dozen police cars are parked, Desper appears at my side blocking my view.

"Your cases are upstairs in the big room overlooking Clay Street. Watch from up there, though there isn't much you can see.

"Please, walk in front of me. Mr. Clayton doesn't want busy bodies to see you until he can talk to you."

"Why was Mr. Dialman's body in my house?"

"My guess, Miss, is because it's been sitting vacant all these years. The lock on the side door is bad…easy entrance."

"Who knows about the door?"

"Good question for which I don't have an answer."

"Please, fix it."

"You're right. When Charity gets back I'll go get a replacement. It'll keep out unwanted after dark visitors."

Like his wife, he has a wicked dry humor. I giggle.

"Desper, was he in the library when I arrived last night?"

"Don't have any way of knowing the answer to that either. You slept through the storm. Didn't know the electricity was off.

"Mr. Dialman wasn't a big man, but he weighed close to 200 pounds. Whoever carried him across the street didn't leave any footprints in the garden. Billy Ray looked real hard so we have to assume he came before the rain."

Their reasoning doesn't calm my fears. My classes in criminal investigation are getting first hand experience. Though I admit a curious disassociation, as if I'm watching a movie and can't keep track of the plot.

~ ~ ~

35

Climbing the stairs and looking down, I stagger as a dizzy spell shakes me to the core. I cling to the banister for support and sit down on a step until it passes. Through the spindles there is nothing in the hall except the diamond pattern of the tiles.

A chill dances along my arms.

I'm glad Desper has gone to finish the lawn. Matron's cold voice echoes in my ears, "*Stop dithering and making a ninny of yourself. Go do as you're told.*"

My quirky laughter bounces on the stairs. The strong coffee, endless tea, and big breakfast has set my stomach to churning. I'd been flippant with Charity to hid my misgivings. The fact remains I no longer have a guardian to tell me what to do.

I'm struck by the insight. I've rarely seen him, yet I depended on him for help.

Any spending money I had arrived in cryptic notes from him. He paid my bills. Never knew how to contact him.

Now I must do for myself.

I sit here contemplating the questions in the silence of the hall. There is so much I don't know.

Who am I?

Where did I come from?

Why is it no one wants me to be seen?

The roar of a lawnmower outside puts an end to my foolish navel gazing.

I climb the stairs to find the room where Desper put my meager belongings to clean away the travel stains.

~ ~ ~

Lug my knapsack to the bed. It's heavy because I'd stuffed a few leftover books in with extra clothes. Boating clothes will do for the present as all I'll be doing is unpacking and exploring since I'm cooped up until I talk to Clayton Forrester.

I fling stuff out on the bed, digging for my favorite outfit. Brown packets emerge from the bottom of the bag. I put them to one side. I need a shower before I can tackle those papers with a clear head.

The attached bathroom is nice and roomy. I make myself at home, scattering my stuff around on the sink. A long hot shower is pure indulgence, but it's my house and I can do as I please. Dry of and tame the wet hair kinks. Then pull on worn jeans and a Navy T-shirt one of the cadets had given me when we got soaked out on the bay.

It doesn't take long to unpack and stow the clothes I plan to keep. A Sunday dress suit I don't like and three pairs of jeans look lonely hanging it a big closet.

My week's worth of cotton underwear is forlorn in the tall chest standing between two wall lamps with cranberry glass shades. Even standing on tiptoes I can't see into the top two drawers. I drag a chair over…they're for jewelry. My silver cross pin from high school and the Navy insignia tie tack I'd picked up on the parade ground are lost on the velvet lining.

Clayton had given me a pair of gold studs after I had my ears pierced in high school. The sisters had a hissy fit when they discovered what we were doing after vespers and lights out. We were on restriction for a month and they informed our parents, in my case my guardian.

I hate the white cotton blouses and navy skirts I've worn in one form or another my entire life. It's like they're tattooed on my skin. I don't want to ever see a Peter-Pan collared blouse again. Same is true for the two pleated wool skirts that hang below my knees and a Sunday summer jumper. I gather the pile in both arms and pitch them over the banister to take out to the garbage.

A quick reconnaissance down the hall reveals three more bedrooms, another bathroom, a linen closet with a clothes chute, and French doors opening out on a porch above the backyard.

A high brick wall surrounds the area. The wall is attached to the garage and broken by a gate. The view is fantastic as if I'm standing in a tree house.

Odd, from up here I can see the freshly mowed grass, which doesn't disguise the tire tracks of a heavy vehicle.

Billy Bejaysus, Mr. Dialman's body was bought to my house by car, right up to the back steps. Any fool can see it from above.

I'm shaking with anger. How dare anyone have the audacity to use my home as their dumping ground for stiffs?

I march back down the hall. It's time to take a closer look at those packets. I know one contains the deed and money I saw last night, but where did the second come from?

More importantly how did they get in my knapsack?

Who in the shades of Hades is playing games with me?

~ ~ ~

Across the way, the police are packing up their gear and leaving. Desper and Billy Ray Johnson are standing in the middle of the street talking. Neither of them seems too happy.

I can't hear what they're saying. Johnson gets in his cruiser, waves to Desper and drives away.

I pick up the fat packet and tear it open. Bank paid utility receipts, in my name, are the first items. I'm horrified at the amounts. They crumble in my fist. I open my hand and let them fall on the bed. Like a somnolent zombi I stagger to the chair by a dainty ladies' desk and spread the papers out.

A certificate of live birth from Kings Daughter's Hospital dated February 14, 1958 for a baby girl, Vivian Philips Dialman. Her parents are listed as Clara Vivian Towbridge and Robert Philips Dialman.

Billy Bejesus, was the Mr. Dialman in the library the same person? Where is his daughter?

Another blue paper wrapped document answers one question. They're formal adoption papers of Vivian by Marcus Laurence McIntyre dated December 8, 1961 with her name changed to Petra Isolta McIntyre. It has notary seals, registry stamps, and witness signatures. They were filed at the courthouse in Ono County, Kentucky by Elton Fightmaster.

The search of a lifetime tied up tight and legal. This is me.

I grab the deed packet off the bed. The signatures match. Elton Fightmaster prepared the deed for the house from Marcus McIntyre's estate to me on December 28, 1964. Three years after the adoption.

What happened?

Why have I been kept secret all these years like I didn't exist?

Wait a minute, the fake birth certificate for Brenda Curtis Burton is dated February 14, 1957. All my school registration forms give 1958 as the year I was born, which makes me 21. If the other paper is correct then I'm 22 years old.

Why the discrepancy?

I shake my head trying to jar loose memories I cannot bring into focus. Every time I try to force my mind to go back it becomes dark. A black void closing in on me.

Clayton Forrester dropped me by the gate. My earliest memory of him is when he told me to walk up the drive to where friends were waiting for me. New shoes were pinching my feet as I stumbled up the gravel road to the big house with my elephant and a small suitcase two months before my fifth birthday.

He lied. The people there were never my friends. They took the suitcase and Dumbo. Left me alone.

The fake birth certificate must have been in my suitcase. Florence Emmens slammed it in my hand saying, "It doesn't have your name on it, but this came with you," when Clayton removed me from the home to attend high school at Cardome Academy, a Catholic boarding school, outside of Georgetown, Kentucky.

As I was getting in the taxi to take me to the train station the gardener passed me a paper sack.

Dumbo was inside. I've never again let him be taken from me. The grey velvet elephant has been my companion for many long nights. He is the only thing I possess that binds me to a life before I was abandoned by the gates to the children's home.

Another taxi met me at the depot and dropped me two blocks up the street at the Breaks Hotel here in Capital City. It was the first time I ever had a room of my own.

Clayton was waiting for me. It's obvious now, he didn't want Mrs. Emmens to know where I was going.

The girl I shared a room with at the academy, entered the cloister after graduation so I don't have any contacts to exchange letters with and get news of others I knew. Most of the students left after a semester or a year. I was one of the few who lived there for four years including the vacation periods, while the others went home.

When I was awarded the scholarship to St. John's College the Mother Superior was delighted.

The day I saw I made the dean's list in the school's organ I realized I'd never received a grade slip.

I went to the Provost's office and learned from one of the student clerks, I was a private pay student. There was no scholarship. It was all an elaborate ruse.

It was a strange existence. The other students were never more than casual acquaintances I would see in classes or pass in the halls.

Girls were few and we didn't have anything in common. The friends I made were on the docks who passed me off as someone's kid brother who loved boats. I took to the hard work. My hands blistered and burned until they harden enough to handle the ropes without flinching.

Out on the water, I was free. Past, future, and present blended into a ghostlike now. Nothing else was important.

My chest tightens as I try to breathe. No more tears.

It's anger.

Anger at being left in the dark, to stumble around, never knowing who I am or where I belong.

My entire life has been searching for a me. A place without the shackles of a hidden benefactor. The deed says the house is mine.

I have a home.

Why has no one told me?

Can I afford to keep it…the utility bills are enormous.

Any extra money I earned or was given to me went to pay tuition to the University of Maryland for a degree in criminology. Initially to learn techniques to discover my own identity. As time went on I became fascinated with the work.

I pull out a wide drawer in the desk. To get the papers out of my sight I shove them in. Or try to. They won't fit. I take them out and feel around the back.

A tarnished silver case is wedged in the back. Its hinges open to reveal a small pair of ornate opera glasses.

The lenses are cloudy with grim. Dumbo is huge when I peer through them. The lenses are deceptive both in their size and power.

I put them in my pocket to clean in the kitchen.

The phone is ringing downstairs. Charity is out getting groceries.

To save time I slide down the banister to get to the phone before the caller hangs up.

~ ~ ~

"Who is Evan Blade?"

"Not sure how to answer."

"What do you mean?"

"Officially, he's a private investigator who works out of a back alley down by the river. A tough guy sort of like the old movie private dicks. Soft spoken. You'll never words like 'broad' or 'moll' come out of his mouth. Best way to describe him is a mass of contradictions."

"Officially?"

"Well…he has slippery clients. TT Towbridge for one, who never did an honest thing in his life. Got his-self elected Lieutenant Governor. Some say he is banking on the top job. Not someone you want to mess with.

"On the other hand, Evan has A plus bonafides. Maddy Sorals acts as his secretary. You call her if you want to find him. Lieutenant Colton of the state police is a friend, straight arrow as they come.

"Desper once told me he thought they're joined at the hip.

"What's your interest in him?"

"He called while you were out. Asked me out for a late lunch."

"Evan Blade? He sees Sheba Cross when he is in town. Man's best friend. Often wondered what astrology sign she was born under. It sure wasn't 'No Trespassing.' She'll not appreciate him taking you to lunch."

"Said Mr. Forrester sent him."

"Possible. Makes sense. He is too old for you to be a real date. Clayton Forester is another of his clients. What is the problem?"

"I don't have anything to wear."

Chapter 7

Planned to have a long lunch at Bihn's, as I haven't had breakfast. Best place in town to catch up on the local scuttlebutt. Something's always buzzing in Capital City.

Good chance to pickup side work to keep my paws in the hopper. Been a cold spell with nothing much in the offering except repos. Come tax time they are a flutter when guys can't meet the payments. For those jobs I take either Wedge or Anvil to discourage an unsatisfied deadbeat from taking a poke at me. Towbridge's work is little more than to keep me on his hook.

Instead, I'm delegated to take a kid out to lunch, big deal. Wonder what burger joint she'll choose.

Maddy's serious about someone wanting to take her out. What kind of low-life would hurt a kid? My parents were carney folks who dumped me in Creelsboro down in Ono County. They didn't mean any harm. I was more baggage than they could cram in their car.

Park the current Whoof with Maddy. She doesn't mind and the dog sure didn't. Her place's his next favorite after the middle of my bed. Every dog I've ever had carries the name Whoof. It was my first word according to Thornton after he got a puppy to keep me company.

When I'm on a job, I drive an old nondescript dinged Dodge Charger. I keep it in the warehouse beside my inside office door. Four coats of primer paint fades it into the local landscape at night. Surveillance work's best conducted with a shield of darkness. My parents did teach me to work the midway from the shadows.

McIntyre's house fronts on Talbott. Looks different from the office side on Clay Avenue. A deep porch runs across the front with a wide swing, scattered wicker chairs, and big pots of ferns.

An old hand crank brass bell is embedded in the oak of a fancy door behind the storm door. I give it a whirl and the door pops open.

The kid stands there dressed in a plain green dress wearing high heeled shoes. She wobbles a bit as she steps back to open the door wider.

"Don't ever open a door unless you know who's on the other side."

How in the hell am I to protect an idiot who flings wide a door on the street?

"Mr. Blade, I watched you drive up. Charity Sims told me who you were.

"I believe you made a luncheon date."

The kid looks at me out of haughty honey colored eyes and doesn't bat an eyelash, as if we've never met.

Motion toward the door and to save face growl, "Let Charity or Desper answer the door."

She nods her head and looks down at her feet.

As we come down the steps she places a hand on my arm. Not flirting, but to keep her balance walking. This kid has never worn women's shoes.

Where has Clayton had her stashed? I can see a tan line around her neck, which says she has spent time outdoors. Faint lines at the corner of her cat shaped eyes show squinting against glare off water.

How old is she?

Last night she looked like a ten-year-old. Today it would take a blind man not to see a full grown woman, even if it's miniature.

When we get to my truck she opens the door and uses both hands to vault into the seat. No stranger to trucks that sit high on the springs.

"Where do you want to eat?"

"You choose. I'm not familiar with Capital City."

"Are you old enough to go where booze's served?"

"Yes."

"Can you prove it?"

"I have a Maryland driver's license."

"Serafini? Best place in town for Italian."

"Fine and after we eat you're to take me to Whipple's."

"I will not."

"Maddy Sorals said you'd be glad too."

I'll wring her neck. Me, in a place so fancy the Queen of England shopped there when she visited her horses in Versailles. It was in all the papers.

"I heard they only take customers by appointment. You don't drop in."

"I know. Mrs. Whipple came to the house and fitted this dress. While we eat she is putting together summer clothes for me. She has a cousin, in New York, who can make shoes to fit. She got these from her window display and they're too big."

Be interesting to know what Maddie has on the Whipples to get them to do her bidding. Like it or not it looks as if I'm going shopping.

~ ~ ~

The kid orders a plate of pasta with pesto sauce. lamb chops, salad, and a beer. She takes eating seriously, no chatter. Little she might be, still she manages to put herself on the outside of the grub like a starved organ grinder's monkey.

Picking up a napkin to wipe her mouth I noticed the inside of her hands. They're calloused and scared with dozens of little slices.

I pick up a hand and turn it over.

"How'd you get these?"

She pulls it back. Face flushes. Hides them in her lap. Then puts both up on the table, turning them with palms up, as if they're a badge of honor.

"Handling the ropes."

"What ropes?"

"Rigging for the sails of a yacht.

"The scars are from shucking oysters. After I learned, I could do it faster than the cadets."

"Where did you learn to sail?"

"Annapolis, where I went to school."

"Navel academy?"

"No, no. You have to be appointed by a senator to get in there. I could watch their drills if I climbed a tree in Mrs. Strove's backyard."

Silly grin flashes across her face and then freezes.

I turn my head to follow her line of sight. Duncan Abbott's standing behind me about to put his hand on my shoulder. Stopped the action with a glare, which leaves his hand dangling in the air, like a limp rag.

"Mr. Towbridge is looking for you. Wants to see you right away. Having lunch with your sister?"

"No."

Ignore him whenever possible. He's too busy polishing TT's boots to be his own man.

It's rumored he has an interest in young girls. Make a point of not introducing him to the kid and field him off.

"My cousin. In town for the day. Got drafted to show her the sights before she catches a train."

The kid sticks out her hand, then drops it.

"I'm Brenda Burton, Mr…"

"Abbott. Hate to spoil your afternoon. Blade has a job he needs to see to immediately. I'm free to give you the tour?"

"Thanks for the message. I'll give him a call after I park her with my aunt."

"Brenda, let's go."

Almost stumble over the change in the moniker.

~ ~ ~

"Miss McIntyre, why the name change?"

"You look like Ansel Adams."

"Who?"

"A famous photographer. The broken nose. Same profile."

Her eyes gleam with silent laughter. It's payback time for calling attention to the scars on her hands.

"Mr. Blade, you lied. I followed suit. I didn't like the man. He was…condescending."

"Likes to feel important. He's Towbridge's errand boy."

"Charity mentioned a Mr. Towbridge."

"Dialman was his…uncle-in-law. Not sure about the terminology, close enough. Abbott's married to Towbridge's niece. He wants to make sure Dialman's murder doesn't cause problems for his political ambitions."

"Oh, I see."

"Yes, having a murder or murderer among one's near and dear can cast a bad reflection on the Lieutenant Governor, even he can't afford."

"What are you going to do?"

"Exactly what I told Abbott. Towbridge's not above having me followed. I'm depositing you at Whipple's. While you're trying on clothes, I'll beg the use of their phone."

~ ~ ~

The waitress passed me a note under my receipt. Note's from Maddy. Levi Whipple's kind enough to loan me their office when I tell him I need to call her.

> *Clayton conscious. I'm to go to the Stoddard Veterinary Clinic after dark. Use the back door.*

Perfect. Have to hand it to the lady. Big animal hospital has all the facilities to treat a gunshot and hide the patient.

Kid's polite, but firm in her choice of clothes. A nice navy dress with a white collar, she rejects out of hand, saying she'll never wear the color again. She doesn't go for girly-girly things. Bold colors. Vivid against her ivory skin are her choices. Takes three dresses, then goes hog wild with blouses, tailored slacks, and shorts.

She shops without once looking at price tags, finishes her business leaving most of the clothes to be altered, and walks out to my truck, as if I'm her chauffeur.

When we leave I ask her who is paying for the loot. She looks at me in a strange manner and says Clayton Forester takes care of her expenses. He's her guardian.

She ordered a beer and drank it as if it was her normal beverage. He can't be her guardian if she's of age.

He's in a hospital bed in an animal shelter, gut shot while she acts like he's going to come riding over a hill to her bidding.

Like hell.

Chapter 8

"Where have you been?"

"Baby sitting the kid. Cop was waiting at the house when we got back."

"What cop?"

"Billy Ray Johnson."

"Why?"

"They knocked on doors. A neighbor mentioned lights in the house last night. Don't worry, the kid's okay. I shoved her down on floor board and told her to stay. While I was talking to Billy Ray the damn idiot got out of my truck and tore her dress climbing over the back gate. Not tall enough to reach over and flip the latch."

"Clayton is resting. He insists on talking to you. Take Whoof with you so it looks legitimate going in there after hours in case anyone sees you."

"Good idea."

"Where are you going after you talk to Clayton?"

"Back to my place to get out of this suit. It smells of

garlic tomato sauce. Then drop by Bhin's to see if I can pick up any loose talk.

"Abbott was in Serafini this afternoon with his nose twitching. Towbridge demands I stop by his office tomorrow. He's nervous about something."

"Should be. Dialman's wife was his sister. She was murdered shortly before McIntyre."

"What?"

"Before your time. Cold, but still an open case and it won't be long until Johnson makes the connection. He is not stupid. Made the headlines in the *Capital Advocate* when TT threatened to kill his brother-in-law, at her funeral."

"Maddy, what in the hell have you gotten me mixed up in? Two old murders, a new murder, an attempted murder, plus looking after a kid who doesn't care to ask about a former guardian she found shot last night?"

"Since you don't have enough to sink your teeth into I'll give you more bad news."

"Don't slam the door in my face. What?"

"Tomorrow afternoon Miss McIntyre will have a visitor. You will stay out of it, unless there is trouble. Your job is to protect her."

"Who?"

"Jordan Ames."

"New lawyer in Buckston?"

"Yes."

"So. As far as I've heard he's a nice guy. Retired military. Married to a former school teacher. What's the problem?"

"He is also Marcus McIntyre's step-son. He is bringing Mary Laurence, to whisk Clayton back to Ono County and to present Miss McIntyre with a will while he is in town."

"So?"

"That is all Elton Fightmaster told me."

"I don't get it. You know we've got to move Clayton. He will insist on it. You called Fightmaster for help. So what's worrying you?"

"Ames. Didn't know he existed. I don't trust lawyers. We promised Clayton we'd protect his ward. I don't like missing pieces showing up unexpectedly. They always come back to bite you in the ass."

~ ~ ~

A small light glows over a buzzer above the word 'Emergency.'

When I push the button a elderly black man opens the door and beckons to me. He closes and locks it on a chain behind me. His spotless white uniform shouts Maddy's cleaning service.

He leads me down a long hall to a closed steel door.

"Nice dog. One of Puckett's?"

"He's spending the night. Maddy's orders."

"She called. My son and I will be cleaning. He is out in the barns."

He unlocks the door. I step into a huge operating amphitheater with heavy pads lining curved half-walls.

"This is where they treat the horses. Walk around the outside to the door opposite this one. He is in there."

Clayton's room has all the facilities of a VIP emergency room at Miner's Hospital and then some.

"Did you bring some malt?"

His voice's strong. No where near the disjointed mumble of last night.

"Didn't think."

"Just as well. Small bag is a morphine drip. I keep drifting in-and-out. I suspect Doc put a sleep aid in the glucose solution."

"Clayton, who shot you?"

"Don't know. Dark. Came down the river in my cruiser. Hid it in a slue above the dock and climbed the bank. Lights were on in the house. Shot came from above. I was a sitting duck, outlined by the security light on the dock. I went down and rolled off the path into some bushes.

"Waited an hour or so. Made it to the house. Petra was in the kitchen crying. She left. I got in to leave her a note. Meant to get out, instead passed out. Came to she was staring at me. Then you barged in. What has happened since I was bundled out?"

Talking costs him. His eyelids flutter.

Bring him up to date. Not wasting time on details. He's pinching himself to stay awake.

Mutters, "damn drugs."

My anger with the kid and her disregard of him shows.

He gives a soft chuckle.

"Weird, isn't it?"

"Callous."

"Doesn't remember."

"What?

"She was standing over you with your blood dripping from her hand."

"Same as when I found her beside McIntyre with his blood on her hands."

"Mental problem?"

"No. Brain shuts down when confronted by horror. Blocks it out. Psychological amnesia.

"I owed McIntyre. He was a square guy his clients weren't. After he adopted her, something happened. His secrets died with him. He was afraid for her. I agreed to become her guardian two months before he was killed.

"She may have seen his killer. I've managed to keep her hidden. She was twenty-one on her birthday. "

She wasn't lying. Misjudged her because she's so small. Said she had a Maryland driver's license. Logical conclusion when college kids make a habit of carrying fake identification. Seen enough of it when a big time name like Chuck Berry played Club 68 outside of Lebanon.

"You get the job by default. Bring her tomorrow night. I'll tell her what I know. Find the killer before he gets a crack at Petra."

"You won't be..."

"Mary is bringing the calvary."

"Ames, the lawyer?"

"Spook first class. Retired Coast Guard Intelligence."

"Have the twins retrieve the cruiser. Truck and trailer are in the lot across from the River Hotel. Maddy has the keys."

Giving orders. Words coming slower as he fights sleep.

"Make a pallet for Whoof. He is pulling guard duty."

Chapter 9

Charity is deep cleaning the library since the police are finished searching for clues. Desper hauled in some boxes and I'm packing Mr. McIntyre's copious files as best I can. It's a miserable ordeal, dismantling someone's professional life. I don't know one thing about the man who was my adoptive parent.

Try as I can I have no recollection of ever having seen him. The best I can do is put the numerous folders in alphabetical order and paste labels on each box. Charity said there was plenty of room in the attic for them. We'll do the same with all the law books or maybe Desper can find someone who can use them.

The curtains and windows are wide open to let fresh air take away the odor of death. It clings to every surface of the room.

I watch a stranger come up the walk and climb the steps to the door. He is tall, but moves with a sailor's gait while wearing cowboy boots like Mr. Blade's.

The bell rings and Charity motions me to be quiet while she answers the summons. A short while later, she comes back into the library with a curious look on her face.

"Miss McIntyre, a Jordan Ames is here to see you on business. I put him in the parlor.

She walks me across the hall and opens the doors so I can enter. Mr. Ames has his back to me, watching Desper work on the same storm door he replaced yesterday.

"Mr. Ames, you asked to see me?"

He pivots in a precise military step.

"Forgive me, I was wool gathering. My grandmother had the same paper in her dining room."

"Awful isn't it?"

"Hideous."

I giggle and he grins. His grey eyes squint with deep water crevasses. Instantly, I like this man. There is a commanding presence about him that spells security."

"Would you please sit down?

"Charity, do you have coffee in the kitchen?"

"Yes, ma'am."

"I'm sure Mr. Ames would enjoy a cup."

She flees, but doesn't close the door. What does she think will happen with Desper taking the door off the hinges?

"Thank you. Coffee would be appreciated.

"Miss McIntyre, my time in Capital City is limited. I wanted to bring you these papers."

He holds out one of those brown envelopes. My hand shakes as I reach to take it.

"When I first opened a practice in Ono County, Elton Fightmaster helped me acquire a few clients. He sent Robert Dialman to me, to draw up his will."

Charity comes back into the room with a large silver tray. On it are a gleaming silver pot of coffee, sandwiches and iced cakes. The china is both old and fine. It's plain with a silver band around the edge. She makes a production of arranging the service while studying Mr. Ames.

"Will this be all, ma'am?"

"Yes, Charity. Thank you."

Mr. Ames and I make a strange pair, drinking coffee as to the manor born. He in his Hong Kong tailored silk suit and me in a Navel Academy T-shirt and worn jeans. I want to howl with laughter at the absurdity of the situation.

I'm sure he is a Navel officer. What does he want with me?

"I'm retired. Coast Guard."

"How…?"

I'm startled he knows what I'm thinking.

"I can see the question in your eyes? You have an expressive face.

"Have the police come to any conclusion, as to Robert Dialman's death?"

"I have no idea. Charity and I were cleaning up the mess they left when you arrived. The carpeting will have to be replaced. She couldn't get the blood stains out.

"What does his will have to do with me?"

"His will could make things awkward for you since his body was discovered in your home."

"How?"

Billy Bejaysus. I sound like a bad Indian impersonation.

"You're his sole heir."

"I'm what?

"I didn't know the man nor have I ever laid eyes on him alive or dead."

"He was your father. He was afraid he would be charged and convicted of murdering his wife. To help him, McIntyre adopted you and changed your name."

I'm the missing daughter. The 'Vivian' whose name was on the birth certificate Clayton left for me. My head is in a whirl and all I can do is stare at Mr. Ames.

"Miss McIntyre, does Charity have anything stronger than coffee in the kitchen?"

"I guess."

"You need it."

He races from the room. My head is pounding like it does before an approaching storm.

"Here, drink it."

He hands me a tumbler full of an amber liquid.

"It's brandy."

Burns my throat and warms my stomach. I'm cold like I was the night I arrived.

Charity picks up the afghan and places it around my shoulders to stop my shaking. Desper steps through the half-hung door into the room.

Mr. Ames points to chairs.

"Sit. You were listening outside the doors."

His manner is commanding and angry.

"Are you working for Mrs. Sorals?"

Desper answers with a susurrant, but respectful shrug.

"No, Sir. We work for Mr. Clayton."

"Can the dumb nigger act. I've seen his methods. He has zero tolerance for fools. Sit there and listen. I don't have time to repeat what I have to say."

"Miss McIntyre, I'm sorry, I thought you knew." He glances at his watch.

"Where is Evan Blade?"

"I don't…"

"Excuse me, Miss Petra. He went to see Mr. Towbridge."

"Who is he?"

"The Lieutenant Governor, Sir."

"I see."

"Mr. Towbridge's sister was Mr. Dialman's wife. She was murdered before Mr. McIntyre."

Charity moves over beside me and starts rearranging the afghan behind my back.

She whispers one word, "Fangs."

Stands up and returns to the chair beside Desper. She is worse than Matron yelling, "Dithering."

I sit up, square my shoulders and take another gulp of the brandy to settle my stomach, then set the empty glass on the coffee table.

He looks at me with Arctic eyes dancing.

"Miss McIntyre, you've also inherited me as your lawyer. Dialman wasn't wealthy as most people see it. He was more than comfortable. You're not to do or sign anything before I see it.

"When I get back to Ono County, I will file for probate down there where the will was executed. By doing it in this manner we can delay the authorities asking questions you can't answer. It will take several working days for the news of your inheritance to trickle through channels."

"According to the papers Mr. Forrester left with me, I've also inherited Mr. McIntyre's estate. This house was deeded to me when I was five years-old. I'm guessing it was done by the man who sent Mr. Dialman to you. It's the same name."

A lopsided grin breaks across his face, "Crafty old sod knows how to drive spikes in a honeymoon."

"Did he get married?"

"No, I did.

"I hate to drop this on you and run, but I've a pressing obligation. Please read the papers. I'll answer any questions when I return.

"Would you mind if I take a look at the room where Mr. Dialman was found?"

"It's across the hall."

~ ~ ~

"Nice office. It reminds me of Elton Fightmaster's. Mine is in my grandfather's surgery. I envy you those law books. They're expensive."

He looks around and thumbs through the folders I'd placed in boxes.

"What do you plan to do with these?"

"Charity says the attic is nearly empty, so I was going to store them up there."

"I have a better idea. Let me present them to Elton Fightmaster. He'll know what should be kept and what can be thrown away."

He has a positively wicked look in his eyes, like a payback for interrupting his honeymoon. I giggle at the joke and he gives me a broad wink, as he knows I've seen through him.

"What about the law books?"

"Elton has shelves of them."

"No, I meant would you like to have them?"

"Miss McIntyre, there is a fortune here, even on the used market."

"Mr. Ames, they're of no value to me. I have no plans to go to law school. I have two degrees. I'm tired of going to school.

"You could pay me a dollar down and a dollar a month."

"You're kidding."

"Yes and no. The electric bills alone for this house are enormous. You just told me I now have another house to maintain. Unless I find a job very soon, I'm not even sure I can afford to keep this house."

"In six months, when Robert Dialman's affairs are settled you will be very comfortable."

"Doesn't solve the immediate problems. I'm sure we can come to an agreement, on the value of the books, to help both of us. Please take them."

"All right, if you're sure."

"I'm positive. Besides those boxes in the corner are my own books and I have more arriving by freight."

"Where did you go to school?"

"St. Johns and the University of Maryland."

"What field of studies?"

"Humanities and criminology."

"Interesting choice. How do you plan to use your education?"

"When you settle the details of the mess I find myself in I intend to open a detective agency."

"Is your guardian aware of your plans?"

"I haven't seen him for over a year. He didn't bother to come to my graduation. Nor has he shown his face since I arrived."

"Miss McIntyre, he couldn't come. Someone tried to kill him. He was shot the night you arrived."

"He was shot!

"Is he dead?"

"No, tonight we'll take him home to recover."

"May I see him?"

"He is in a private hospital, under guard. Evan Blade will escort you tonight during visiting hours."

He looks at his watch. "I must go. I'm late. It has been time well spent."

~ ~ ~

I walk him to the door. As I watch him drive away, I feel confused and alone, like I've never been in my life. Charity and Desper disappeared to the kitchen. I follow them to escape the emptiness of the house.

They're sitting at the counter with Evan Blade. My temper blazes.

"Why didn't you tell me my guardian was shot? I had to find out from a stranger."

A large black dog comes around the island as I scream at him.

"Whoof, friend."

The dog immediately sits down in front of me and lifts his paw to shake hands. I can't resist and returned his friendly gesture.

I round on Mr. Blade, "You didn't answer my question."

"As we're going to be seeing a lot of each other lets settle a point. My name's Evan.

"Understand?"

"Where do you come off thinking we're going to be seeing each other?"

"Because Brat, Clayton has given me firm orders not to let you out of my sight. When I can't be around, Whoof will be beside you. Maddy will skin me alive and have me for breakfast if anything happens to you. Got it, Bonehead?

"Now eat."

He hands me a thick sandwich.

"Desper told me Ames poured enough brandy down you to stop a horse. You're drunk."

"I am not."

"Charity, warm up the coffee. We've got to talk. I need her full attention."

"Told you. I'm not drunk."

"Tell it to the marines, Kid-do."

"Mr. Blade, stop calling me names."

"Your ears will burn if you knew the names I've been calling you. The name's Evan."

To keep from crying, I eat and endure his tirade. Charity and Desper fill him in on what Mr. Ames told us. He starts pacing the floor, which makes me dizzy.

Chapter 10

Abbott practically drags me down the long hall to Towbridge's office. He'd been waiting outside the gym with a car when I stepped out.

TT's office complete with his heavy-eyed niece seated to the side of the inner sanctum. It precludes power even if it's only at the first louie level.

Not yet eight o'clock and all ready Faith Abbott's three sheets to the wind. Word on the street she's so deep into the sauce Abbott only trots her out for public appearances to avoid talk. Her movements slow…clumsy. She presses a buzzer under the edge of the desk. Abbott pushes me through into TT's office as the thick doors open.

Nice set up. An empty government building on a Sunday morning. His Lincoln was the single car in the parking lot by the side door when we arrived.

The walls are dark wood with shelves full of books. It's questionable TT ever read one. Three paintings of the river, by Paul Sawyer look like originals to my untrained eye or master copies, are scattered around the room.

The state seal hangs behind the desk. I've always thought those two guys should have their hands in each other's pockets instead of shaking them.

He fits behind the long desk as if he'd been born to it. TT on the prowl isn't the same buff friendly fellow he presents to the public.

We both know how he'd gotten there. He knew all the wrong stuff about the right people and hadn't been shy about using it. I'd provided the bulk of his ammunition with background checks on known players. Phone calls and a bit of clandestine surveillance.

Not dependent on TT's dirty work. Doesn't pay the rent though it does keep Whoof in Alpo on feast days.

"Thanks for the ride."

Can't keep the sarcasm out of my voice. Been looking forward to a Charity breakfast before I squire the brat to church. Capital City has one of each denomination pushing on two hundred years old. Never been in one. Don't intend to make a habit of it no matter what orders Maddy passes out.

Charity let drop the brat had gone to high school at a convent so I guess it 'll be Saint Michael.

"Told you yesterday I'd be here. I keep my word. Don't need help from your lackey."

"Duncan, go to the Turleys out on the highway and get us some decent coffee with hot sticky buns. Take Faith with you. She needs the fresh air before going to church. Call in what we want and it will be waiting when you arrive."

His command's said in a soft voice. It's an order none the less. Hands him a twenty as if to say, 'keep the change.'

Abbott looks at me with a question in his eyes. I nod. We both know TT's temper explodes when he appears the calmest. Today he isn't calm. Something's eating him.

Dislikes opposition. Impatient of restraint. Never make a hunter.

Strip the facade to bare bones, the most powerful man in Capital City's so scared his shorts are in a twist.

When Abbott closes the door, it relieves the tension. Shoot TT a simple question.

"Who do you want me to dig for dirt?"

"The bastard who murdered my sister and brother-in-law."

His stiff retort takes me back a step.

"A city cop was in here Friday afternoon making noises. He pitched their deaths in my lap."

"Billy Ray Johnson?"

"Yes."

"He's slow. Persistent when he gets a bit between his teeth."

"He is off base. I didn't kill or have them killed. I've spent the past sixteen years badgering the State boys to keep my sister's death an open case. They have orders to inform me of any new developments. Now Robert turns up in McIntyre's kid's house…shot.

"If I hadn't been sitting in this chair he'd have accused me…me of murder.

"I had Robert worked over when Clara died. He didn't do it. They had a daughter. Cute little tyke. During the confusion of her mother's death she disappeared. Robert swore he didn't know what happened to her.

"He was a proud man. I was angry. I never got a chance to apologize. He wouldn't take my calls."

"I don't do heavy stuff. It's out of my league."

"You're a detective. You aren't wired into city channels, but you know the players. What is Johnson…a rookie cop? He wasn't wearing a uniform."

"The city police force's small. Top jobs are passed down through inheritance. Johnson's a local football hero who couldn't pass the physical for the State Police because of a bum knee. He has been around for over ten years. Does the grunt work under a title of investigator then one of the chosen few gets the credit."

"Don't try to pawn me off with nonsense. Before you changed your name you blew an outstanding career in law enforcement."

Bastard. TT's so deep in a major crises he has Abbott haul me into his office on a Sunday morning. He doesn't know any method except blackmail.

He has let his anger overplay his hand. I buried that life along with a few friends twelve years ago.

Give him the blank look I'd perfected for cops on the midway.

Best warn Maddy she has a turncoat working both sides of the street.

"I need someone I can trust. Someone I know."

"I see."

The truth of the matter's neither of us knows or trusts the other.

"How well do you know Johnson?"

"Traded favors over the years. We both workout at the gym with some would be punks from the Bottoms who could graduate into real problems. Hate to see kids get their tickets punched, now the draft isn't hanging over their heads to straighten 'em out, before they've time to make major mistakes."

"The State has plans for a hotel complex in the area."

"What happens to the people who live and work down there? Most of 'em have been around as long as your family. Just never made it across the tracks."

"Blade, I don't know. The Governor's project. He is seeking Federal Flood Control monies and playing it close to the vest. He is from the Four Rivers area down state and an outsider to Capital City. He owes a few developers, who sank big money into his election, and he is hungry to appoint himself senator, if the old guy kicks off during his term."

"Hate to see Grundy's go. Only place to get genuine cornbeef or Ruben sandwich."

"True. I despise barbecued mutton. I've eaten a lot of it lately and smiled. Guy from Dawson Springs does the smoking. Catered the White House when Johnson was in office."

Buzzer sounds. Abbott enters carrying a big box while his wife holds the door.

"Put it on the table by the window.

"It's nice out. Take yours and go eat in the park across the street. Then catch the early service. I'll drop Blade back at his club when we're finished."

Towbridge waves me over to the table. Abbott looks at him, nods, picks out their stuff from the box and heads for the door. The box holds an extra large thermos of coffee. He stands at the window and watches until I see Abbott and his wife cross the street.

"Dig in. Cold coffee tastes like varnish remover."

The phone rings as he lifts his paper cup. He hurries over to the desk to answer while I study on how to eat a sticky bun, without getting it on my best suit.

Influence doesn't count for much if a cloud of murder hangs over your head. Towbridge isn't admitting it. Shows in the way he keeps clicking a ball point pen as he talks.

Power mongers run for cover at the first sniff of trouble. Move on to less tainted pastures. Billy Ray's visit during business hours, for all to see, has tarnished TT's image. Bad move on Johnson's part.

"Sorry for the interruption. Golf foursome for this afternoon has been canceled."

Starting. Lieutenant Governor has a problem on his hands which may get too hot for him to handle. Takes a bite of a sticky bun big enough to choke a mule and doesn't get a drop of the runny icing on his fingers. Glad I wasn't the smuck who delivered the slight. Someone will pay.

Against my better judgement I relent because, for a brief moment I feel sorry for the guy.

"Murder isn't my forte. Haven't touched anything heavy in years. Only thing I can do is ask around about Dialman's death as it relates to my current case."

"You work for me. What case?"

Look him straight in the eye. He doesn't flinch and is genuinely puzzled. Towbridge's methods may be dubious, even down right crooked, if the price is right. About family, he is firm. He lives by *nepotism is a good system as long as you keep it close to home*.

Give him information he doesn't have to make sure I have his full attention.

"Baby sitting Clayton Forrester's ward. He was shot down by the river the night Dialman died."

"Forrester…there was no one admitted to the hospital by that name. Is he dead?"

Damn, his sources are almost as efficient as Maddy's.

"No, he's being taken home. Lieutenant Colton's driving the ambulance."

"Never heard of him. Colton is State Police."

"Capital City isn't Forrester's turf. I met him in 'Nam and owe him. He saved my life on my last flight out of that rotten cesspool."

"I see. Big debt. What is the problem?"

"What I'm about to tell you's for your ears only, so shut off the damn recorder. If one word of this leaks anywhere I will personally come down on you, like a ton of Crenshaw's sand you'll never crawl out from under."

He studies me from behind the coffee cup. I'm not bluffing. No one talks to him as I have. He makes his decision and pulls the recorder from his pocket. I reach over, shut it off, and remove the tape, which I put in my pocket. Then shake out the batteries. Few people, even Lieutenant Governors, remember to carry spare batteries.

"Okay, this is how it unravels. Forrester's ward is Marcus McIntyre's adopted daughter. Someone wants her dead because as a little kid she may have seen his killer. Clayton found her beside his body the night he died."

"There wasn't anything in the papers about a child being present."

"No, he hid her where she wouldn't be found. She's grown now. Finished college at a fancy school on the east coast and deserves to get on with her life."

"What school?"

"Annapolis, St. Johns."

"What! A cousin went there. He works for a place like MIT. He couldn't take the academic load so he transferred to Transylvania."

"This 's where it gets complicated. Yesterday a lawyer, by the name of Ames visited. She's also Dialman's legal heir. She was Dialman's daughter. He asked McIntyre to adopt her after his wife was murdered, when he thought he might go to prison."

"Vivian? She is my niece. I'll go get her."

We both stand.

"No. You will not. You will go about your business as if you don't know one damn thing. Clayton has gone to a lot of trouble to keep her safe from McIntyre's killer."

"But she is family."

Appeal to the only thing he knows. His sense of self-preservation.

"Think. Think hard. The police are sniffing around your door. Dialman was murdered. His body hidden in her house. Her legal guardian was shot below the house. You can't go barging in, waving the flags of this office, claiming she's your niece without one iota of proof.

"What will the police believe?

"You're in a tight spot. One of your golf buddies will have to arrest you on suspicion, if nothing else and hold you for questioning.

"Consider how it will look in the headlines?"

He flops down in the chair. Defeated. A powerful man with his hands tied behind his back.

"The kid's safe. Recovering from too much brandy, which Ames fed her. He thought she knew the score. Whoof's by her side and unless I miss my guess, he spent the night in her bed. Charity and Desper Sims are inside the house. Anvil and Wedge Forge are outside running surveillance."

"Never heard of these people."

"They're the best. Charity and Desper are Clayton's hire, recommended by Maddy Sorals. The twins are my backup men for the heavy stuff I can't handle. They were Army MPs. Got out of 'Nam without being scalped. They're hard men to kill."

He turns. Surveys the clouds. His hands grip the chair arms as if it's going to take flight. Wait out his temper battle.

"Cute. I have a photograph taken with her mother. Funny shaped eyes, sherry-brown with flicks of green and thick curly hair. Didn't look like anyone in the family. She and Faith are the only links I have left to my personal family. Older brother and younger sister are dead.

"Duncan hides it well. Thinks I don't know. Faith is a lush."

Can't get Pi off his mind. Talks about her as if she's still a child.

"How is Vivian?"

"She has one recognizable family trait. After three days in her company I can tell you from personal experience she's a stubborn, obnoxious brat who lies like a trooper.

"Friday, she waltzed into Serafini on high heals, I'll swear she'd never worn, and uses a Maryland drivers license to order a beer. When Abbott found me, she introduced herself as Brenda Burton.

"Physically. Tiny for a full grown woman. Mrs. Whipple's ordering her custom shoes from New York. Asleep, she looks like a little kid hugging a grey elephant."

"Dumbo."

"What?"

He turns and faces me. He's smiling.

"The elephant. I took her to see the Disney movie at the Star Theater. Bought the elephant for her at the concession stand after the show."

"Forrester says she suffers from some kind of psychological amnesia. He found her beside McIntyre with blood on her hands. I found her standing over Clayton with his blood dripping from her hand. Like a stone statue. Not pretending. She doesn't remember the events.

"Bizarre and very real."

"Who is this lawyer, Ames? Is he any good?"

81

"Don't know about his legal qualifications. Maddy vetted him through Elton Fightmaster."

"I know Elton. Ahead of me in law school. First class legal brain, who faces more hell every morning getting dressed than the rest of us will see in a lifetime. Wears a steel brace on his left leg. He had polio as a kid."

"I've never met Fightmaster. Clayton said Ames's retired military."

"Then he'll do right by Vivian?"

"Maybe. He's also McIntyre's step-son."

"Red haired with freckles?"

"Didn't see him."

"Met him at a picnic after we graduated from high school. Not important. I'll see he doesn't cause Vivian problems."

"Her legal name's Petra Isolta McIntyre."

He ignores what I say and gets down to brass tacks. A language he knows well…money."

"Who's footing your bill?"

"Clayton Forrester gave me a healthy retainer. Emptied his wallet to cover my expenses."

"I'll triple his fee plus expenses when you find my sister's killer."

"Your sister's death was before my time. Trail's as burned over as a sword swallower's throat.

"If I'm to take on your problem, I need to know everything. Whole nine yards. Good and the ugly. No protecting the family name.

"It's too late to be noble or pull rank…too many people have been murdered.

"Treasury hasn't printed enough money for me to go into this mess blind then get cut off at the knees if I step on toes, including yours. Let Johnson handle it.

"He's earned a promotion many times over. Needs to crack a big case, to get him inches in the local and state papers, where they're forced to save face and give it to him. Let him work it. Keep my name out of it."

TT sits there looking at me and thinking. He knows I mean what I say and am not afraid of him. He doesn't have the power to harm me. He walks over to his desk and pulls out a worn leather briefcase.

"It's all in here. Every thing I have collected over the years, photos, newspaper stories, autopsy report, interviews of people who knew her, and the police reports."

He hands it to me, flat on both hands like the old case contains the crown jewels. Together we check each folder and its contents. Then I give him a detailed written receipt.

"I'll read everything. Let you know my final decision. I want you to tell me exactly what happened the night your sister died."

"Blade, it was sixteen years ago. You can't expect me to remember every little detail."

"You've never forgotten a detail in your life. Start playing games with me, then I'm out of here."

Chapter 11

A younger version of the old man lets us in the back door of the clinic. Whoof's walking beside Pi as if he belongs to her. The door to Clayton's room's ajar.

Voices are spilling out into the hall. As we come around the curved wall I motion for Pi to keep quiet.

His father stands to the side of the door listening as Maddy trained him to do.

Old man whispers, "Sparks flying. They're in love and don't know it."

He smiles at his son and almost scampers down the hall.

I can hear Mary Laurence reading Clayton the riot act. I have no qualms about eavesdropping. It's pure pleasure to know someone's able to cut him down to human size. Tough guy's play dough where she's concerned.

Pi mouths, "Who?"

"His lady. She's getting him out of town and has marriage on her agenda."

We put our ears to the crack and listen like two kids.

"Do you hear me? I'm not going to bring an illegitimate child into the world."

"They can hear you in the next county. Calm down. You're pregnant?"

"Yes."

"It's my child too. What do you mean you won't have our baby?"

"Clayton, it's as plain as the nose on your face. No marriage. No child. I lived through the hell other kids give a bastard at school. Aunt Ophelia and my grandparents protected me as much as they could. They couldn't stop what went on at school."

The age old hurt of injustice plain in her voice.

"I refuse to do it to one of my own."

"You're running a business. You can't keep working."

"I'm sure there is an empty file draw around the office I can use for a cradle while I'm working.

"Are you going to make an honest woman of me?"

"Mary, that is your problem, you're too damn honest.

"Yes, I'll marry you, but you must un-brick the entrance to the tunnels under your house."

"Why? I didn't close them off in the first place. You and Jordan did it all on your own."

"My work demands I come and go unobserved, even by close friends. I'm not lying in this hospital bed because someone wants me to live to a ripe old age.

"We'll live at my place?"

Living arrangements seems like as good a place as any to open the door.

"Anyone home?"

Mary's sitting on the edge of the bed. Her hair tousled. Her lips puffy, as if she's been soundly kissed. Her blush's fantastic when she spots Pi hiding behind me. She darts across the room to a mirror.

Clayton grins and beckons to Pi, who has become strangely quite as she takes in the heart monitor and tubes running into Clayton. I learn something. The brat has never seen a real hospital room. She doesn't know how to act or what to say.

Almost laugh when they both say, "I'm sorry."

Whoof breaks the ice by raising up and putting his paw out to Clayton.

He ruffles the thick fur around his collar, shakes hands, and points to the pallet.

"Your place is over there. Does he always sleep with you?"

"After I'm down for the night, except for the cot you've got above the garage. He dumped us both on the floor."

"Don't have much time before the doctor arrives to give me a shot. He wants me out during the trip, as a precaution against injury. I dumped his happy pills in the drinking glass. Those things scare me to death.

"Pi, I don't have a choice to leave this charming facility. I'm at the mercy of a scheming woman who intends to keep me alive until I put a ring on her finger. Mary Louise Laurence, I'd like for you to meet my ward, Petra Isolta McIntyre."

There's no getting around it even in a wrinkled dress with finger combed hair Mary Laurence's one beautiful woman. Added to her classical features 's the inner glow women get when they're expecting. Her simple smile directed to Pi's warm and welcoming.

"When it's safe we're taking him to the lake house to recover. He pretends getting shot is nothing out of the ordinary. This one almost killed him. I intend for him to live so I can watch him explain to our child why Daddy has so many scars."

Her blue eyes are dancing as she teases Clayton, but the tension she has lived with for the past days, shows in the way she holds her shoulders, stiff and prepared to fight to protect her man.

"Pi, I don't have much time so I want you to pay close attention. Legally, you're no longer my ward. Your well being is still bound to the promise I made to Marcus. You're to follow Even's instructions to the letter."

"But…"

"No buts. George Stanolopis and Juan Torres are not here to watch your back or warn amorous cadets to back off when you take it into your head to snag rides, as a cabin boy on sailboats."

"You used my friends to spy on me. How dare you?"

"You were my ward. I couldn't, and still can't, be around all the time. I made a promise to a fine man to watch over his adopted daughter and keep her safe. I keep my promises."

Clayton squeezes Mary's hand. He doesn't take those changeable hazel eyes from Pi.

She stands by his bed like a Bantam rooster, with her hands fisted on her hips ready to fight all comers. There isn't any question as to who's going to win this clash of wills. It's fun to see the brat taken down a peg or two.

Catch Mary's eye, she's enjoying the show.

"You don't have to keep watching me. I'm living in my own house. I haven't seen a male my age. I can't sail on a muddy old river. What can happen?"

"Let me remind you. Mr. Dialman died in your library and I was shot outside. Someone intends to evict you. Jordan Ames filled me in on your new inheritance. How long do you think it will be before the police come knocking on your door asking questions?"

"I was in Maryland."

"You were in the house. Don't lie, especially to the police. I saw you. Your car is hard to miss. It was on the street by the gate until Evan moved it. If I saw it your neighbors may have seen it."

"All the houses were dark, except Mr. Dialman's. I looked."

"Doesn't mean someone wasn't standing behind a shade looking out to see what car came up their quiet street."

"My car doesn't make noise."

"Stop right there. You're being obstinate. I don't have either the time or patience for long discussions while you come up with 'buts'.

"Some spending spree you went on at Whipple's. What happened to your clothes?"

"I threw those ugly school clothes away. I hated them."

Mary squeezes Clayton's hand and he gets the message. It's a female thing she understands.

"I see. How's your money holding out?"

"She didn't ask for any money?"

"Mary, please give Blade the briefcase. Take care of the bill. I don't want outstanding obligations pending. Should be enough to last until I get back on my feet."

Take the case from her and place it on the floor by my feet. Whoof moves beside it.

"Evan, escort her to Southern Trust and have her sign signature cards for the household and personal account. The bank pays the bills. She'll need food and supplies.

"Pi, Dialman was trying to do right by you after his wife gave you to Marcus McIntyre. His death and its circumstances have put you in a bad position. I imagine his relatives will not be pleased to learn there is a new heir."

"I don't want his money."

"Beside the point, according to Jordan, it was all yours as of the day of his death. Unlike McIntyre's will there was no 'of age' clause and between the two of them you're an extremely affluent young woman.

"Along with money, you've inherited a family, one of whom is our current Lieutenant Governor. The story around town is, as a kid TT Towbridge got his spending money from the church collection plate."

One I've never heard. How did Clayton come by it?

A man, I assume must be Ames from his description, opens the door, looks back over his shoulder and enters looking impatient.

"Mary, the ambulance driver frisked me."

Start laughing. He's on the job.

"You met Lieutenant Curtis Burton Colton, State Police Homicide Division and Ono County native."

"With that string of surnames you didn't have to add the last." He grins and sticks out his hand.

"Blade, I presume.

"I'm Jordan Ames. We'll talk later. It's getting late, Mary."

A small neat man wearing thick glasses and carrying a worn leather bag enters the room. I pull Pi away from the bed. Ames joins us out of the way of the professional.

Place's beginning to look like a Marx brothers' skit.

Ames glances at his watch.

"This has to be timed so our caravan doesn't meet the city police on their rounds.

"Miss McIntyre, I'm driving Mary behind the ambulance. I'll get some sleep and come back as soon as I can. Take care of her, Blade."

We follow him out the door. Curt gives me the high sign, but stays behind the wheel.

As they're loading him in the ambulance, Clayton stops 'em and beckons me over to the gurney. His eye lids are fluttering like they did the other night.

He clasps my hand and passes me a small envelope that once held pills.

"Forgot to tell you. Dialman owned the farm where the twins anchor their marina. Makes her your landlady."

"Keep her out of trouble. It has a way of finding her."

Chapter 12

It's late when I get back to the warehouse. Check the far end where Maddy has her flop house for wandering derelicts and outcasts. No one asks questions and Sam runs the show. A small man somewhere between forty and sixty with the personality of a masochistic drill sergeant.

"Got a new one tonight."

He points to the far back corner where a kid stares at me from swollen eyes. He's clutching a battered comic book while trying to blend into the wall. Bottoms written all over him.

Knew him. Seen him hanging around the gym, though not giving the hoops a go as kids will do. His battered eyes saying he's somewhere between twelve and a hundred on the scale of experience.

Been him for a week or so, back when I'd loved the wrong woman, trusted a partner, and killed a innocent man in a fight. Curt Colton rescued me and dumped me on Elroy Harris and Lon Chambers. They dried me out then put me on a bus to California, into the hands of a rabbi and priest who'd make Sam a patsy for a soft touch.

Two years later, I returned to Capital City with a new name, new papers including a West Virginia birth certificate which I'd never had, a California PI license, some schooling, and a worked over face. It'd been too late to fix my nose.

"Worth saving?"

"Reckon."

"Take care of him."

Maddy stocks the place with leftovers from motel and hotel rooms. She uses a backroom for clean clothes patrons left behind. I slip in to pillage a fresh shirt and underwear.

"Bring your stuff over before you leave. I'll drop it off at the laundry and pick it up."

I dig out a couple of twenties and hand them to him. It's a service I've learned to appreciate over the years. Fresh clothes isn't a fetish in my profession. It's a job requirement.

Maddy says laundry costs won't fly with the IRS as an expense, though it seems reasonable to me. Who wants to do business with a smelly detective?

Put a kettle on to boil for tea, feed Whoof, turn a fan on low, strip and remake the bed with fresh sheets, set the tea to brew then shower.

When finished, I have two pillow cases stuffed with dirty clothes plus two suits and a sports jacket. I tote my stuff over to Sam before I make a cornbeef sandwich and a glass of iced tea. These I take outside to a rough log bench and spool table above the river, to mentally replay the day while

Whoof takes his final run for the night.

Monsignor Bryan Stanley and Ben Lehman instilled in me habits which have served me well. If there's a job I don't like to do, never go to bed with it hanging over my head.

Each night when I'm working a case I review the day mentally while I relax and have a snack. Get out my notes to fill in blanks, pull the typewriter over to the desk and write a rough summary of the day. Later when the case's closed or fizzles out I polish my diary to issue a final report for the client.

Then tackle the hard stuff. Tonight there are two brief cases on the floor by my desk. Clayton's money can wait.

Scan the yellowing newspaper clippings. Only a few include the banner of the paper. I assume the ones that don't were taken from the local rag.

Crime scene photos are poorly lite and grainy, but the folder does contain an envelope of original negatives in glassine protective sleeves. If I need to, I can have the printing wizard at Photo Shots have a go at them.

Autopsy report from the state crime lab. Detailed down to the wine Clara Dialman had prior to the attack. She'd been worked over with fists before having her neck broken by a culprit wearing gloves. Report gives the time of death as between eight and ten PM.

Earrings had been ripped from her ears and her neck showed cut marks which indicated a necklace had been jerked from her neck after she died. Their conclusion was the robbery was committed after her body was dumped by the river, as there was no blood around the wounds.

City police had done a yeoman's job of canvassing seventy-five or so people who attended the dinner. Their reports included names and addresses with brief statements substantiating Towbridge's story. He told it, as if it was a recording he'd repeated many times.

It was his first time to speak to a large group and his initial state wide race. In the fall he was running for Commissioner of Agriculture, where he had no opposition. A four year nothing job that provided an introduction to state operations. An apprenticeship to the real workings of state government.

He'd wanted to run for Commonwealth Treasurer. Had been advised not to waste his time or risk his career going against Alexandra Stevens, with her powerful big city backing.

He'd arrived in the ballroom around 6:30 to check-out the microphone hook up at the podium, to make sure they didn't squall when turned on. Dialman came in about 6:45 to help him make adjustments so his talk would go smoothly.

Towbridge was a guest speaker at the Capital City Women's Club dinner in the upstairs ballroom of the Breaks Hotel to raise funds for a project his sister was heading. Her husband arrived about 15 minutes late without his wife. He said she had broken the heel on her shoe and sent him on to pinch hit for her while she repaired the shoe.

They were seated on the podium. Dialman on his right and the President of the Club, Monica Van der Meir to his left facing the audience. Chair on the end was turned up for his sister. Club president suggested Dialman move over to take Clara's original seat so the vacant space wouldn't show to the audience, so she could slip in and not cause a disturbance while everyone was eating.

After dinner TT gave his speech. He and Dialman worked the room, chatting with friends and meeting new people until nearly eleven o'clock. When asked, he made polite excuses for Clara's absence as Faith Abbott (his niece) had suffered a miscarriage, that afternoon after a fall down the stairs.

They left the ballroom and adjourned to the hotel bar for a night cap to rehash his speech. Dialman at this point was nervous and worried about Clara, though he didn't think it was more than a ploy on her part to skip a boring evening, which she was prone to do.

Her body was found by early morning riders exercising their horses. The body was off the path wedged against a pier of the Singing Bridge above the Capital City Yacht Club.

~ ~ ~

Entire file's as dull and stale as Towbridge's statement, but supported by seventy-five people. As it stood, it was impossible for either him or his brother-in-law to have had anything to do with Clara Dialman's death. From force of habit, I go back and study the inadequate crime scene photos.

Soft soil's churned by what I now know are horses hooves and of little use. Her body's against the stone piling of the bridge, near but not in the water. Her feet are closest to the camera, hence the perspective's elongated. Knowing the location, the photographer would need to have been standing on a ladder in thin air to have gotten a better shot.

Start to turn it over to go to the next shot, when it hits me.

Clara Dialman's wearing shoes.

Hard to tell from the photo, but I think one heel's broken. Take a squinting look through a magnifying glass. The heel of her left shoe's crooked, difficult to be sure. Pete Donahue will have to work his magic with a blowup for it to be conclusive.

Towbridge told me in his office and in his statement to the police, Clara had broken the heel getting in the car. No, getting in the car was in Dialman's statement. All TT had said was she had broken her heel.

Her killer had to have grabbed her before she got back to the house. Where was she during the two hours when

Dialman left for the dinner and when she died?

Put the envelope of negatives in my suit pocket to take by Photo Shots in the morning. Place everything else back in the briefcase and stow it in my safety deposit box above the false ceiling tiles accessed by putting a stool in the middle of my desk.

Open Clayton's briefcase to count the lettuce to write a receipt.

Money.

Lot of it in various denominations and several different currencies. It's the brief note, a loaded Luger, and a packet of papers that terrorize the hell out of me down to unraveling my socks if I'd been wearing any.

> *All the cash I could lay my hands on.*
>
> *The papers open vaults TT doesn't*
>
> *know exist. You've been in my employee since*
>
> *you left Ca. Used them myself-your nose*
>
> *is hard to duplicate. Put safe place.*
>
> *Ames will fill you in on particulars.*

Look around to see if anyone's watching before it dawns on my stunned consciousness, my working office space doesn't have windows. The steel door's locked. Clayton had helped me design security when I opened shop. He'd joke and said irate husbands were hard on detectives who supplied their spouses with evidence for a divorce.

Hands shake as bad or worse as when I had DTs, as I study the packet of papers.

Valid New York driver's license and passport. Photos had been taken when I was in California and wearing what passed for a beard by the cameraman, Kasin Ioto. Ben Lehman had him teach me photography. Still have the plaid shirt.

Passport had been used as recently as last year for entrance to Portugal and other countries where I've never been.

There's a key to a safety deposit box located in a Cincinnati bank with a copy of a card bearing the signature I'd made when practicing signing my new name.

Two things remain from my old life: my Social Security number and middle name. I assumed Curt arranged it like he did Army records in 'Nam.

Check book and passbook savings account from Cloverton National Bank, in Allerton County. Each month an Army payroll check's deposited by mail to the savings account.

An account with a stock broker for a non-taxable mutual fund, with a healthy balance.

I'm listed as a member of a below the basement security branch, of the United States Army, with a rank of captain and full security clearances.

Damn it to hell! He'd revoked my discharge. As an officer I can be recalled to active duty at any time. I've seven years to go until I can retire as a thirty-year-man or face a life-term in Leavenworth for fraud.

How did Towbridge find out? Hadn't known myself?

Son-of-a-bitch has been using my identity as a cover in his activities. He's made me a god damn spy sporting an unforgettable face.

Chapter 13

Sleep's a commodity I've had little of, while sitting on the keg of dynamite stashed in the deep safe. It burned a hole thru the concrete to my mattress. Shower and a shave, so close my skin still burns, helped. Not enough to hide a rough night from Curt.

Agreed to meet him for an early breakfast. Don't know how he does it. He'd driven to Allerton County, a good four hour round trip last night.

It's five AM. He's working on a second pot of coffee and dressed to play golf. Windbreaker hides his side-arm. Law requires he carry at all times. Looks sharper than I do wearing a suit and tie.

"Sit down before you fall down. No one followed you to the parking lot or parked across the street. I've been watching."

"How did the trip go? How's the patient?"

Thoughts of undoing the doctor's handy work push their way through my mind, though reason tells me I need Clayton alive, more than ever. At least until he can get me out of the Army and the mess he created in his spook world. Then all bets are off.

"Smooth as silk. He is stashed at Bear Point with Mary holding an old 12 gauge. Ames picked up Doc Flanders to check him over before he woke up from the knock-out shot. Abel Young is next door.

"Abel's next door?"

"Yes, he uses the path on Abel's place to get down the cliff to

his boat house, which he got permission for from the Corp to anchor on their property. To return the favor, he lets Abel and Isaac tie up along side."

"Wait…"

"Evan, Lake Cumberland is owned by the government. They own fifty feet above summer pool, so you must have their permission to have a dock on the lake. It isn't like Tuckingham, where you dock. It belongs to a utility company. Property owners' land goes down to the water line."

"Can anyone get to him from the water?"

"Would take some doing on a lake with over a twelve hundred miles of shoreline. Stop worrying, he is safe. Who shot him?"

"Wish I knew. Clayton told me he didn't see the shooter. I think it's tied in with Robert Dialman's murder."

"City jurisdiction. I can't interfere unless I'm called in and then only on a limited basis."

Pull the small envelope Clayton had given me, out of my pocket.

"Can you do me a favor?"

Hand it to him. Very carefully, he opens it and rolls the bullet onto a fresh napkin. He doesn't touch it. Studies it and looks up at me.

"Where did you get this?"

"Doctor dug it out of Clayton."

"There sure as hell is a connection to the Dialman killing and to the murder of Marcus McIntyre."

"How do you know?"

He takes my pencil and points at the nose of the bullet.

"Bend down and get a close look. See the scars on the nose. Whoever did this is an amateur. Used a little file like a nailfile to make the cross. Too small and not deep enough to work like the TV shows proclaim."

"You said McIntyre's murder. That was sixteen years-ago."

"I may spend sixty percent of my time behind a desk shuffling papers to prepare for teaching training classes, but Joe Taylor at the lab keeps me informed on what turns up in his department.

"Our crime lab is the only one in town. The city sends their stuff to us."

"You're saying both McIntyre and Dialman were killed with the same gun."

"My estimate is the bullets were fired from the same gun by the same person. Don't have the gun to check ballistics, but the monkey work on the bullets is a match. Dialman was still alive when he was hidden in Miss McIntyre's home. He bleed out behind the desk. Maybe the perp didn't know Dialman was still breathing. He'd been worked over before he was shot. I'd say his killer wanted something from Dialman, which he didn't get, so he shot him in frustration. Pure speculation and impossible to prove."

"What?"

"Good question. No telling. Why the obvious staging? It wouldn't fool a ten-year-old. The simple answer is to implicate someone else and throw the police off track."

"Why shoot Clayton? I wasn't in it until Maddy called me. I owe him."

"I understand about Clayton. I was there.

"Murder isn't your turf. How deep are you mixed up in this?"

Our eggs congeal as I tell him about Brat and TT. A ray of the rising sun hits the windshield of my truck, blinding me. We both look at the mess on the table and moved across the room. Order a fresh breakfast.

"Clayton's ward is Towbridge's niece?"

"Seems so."

"He wants her under his protection."

"That's what he said. I held him off until Dialman's murder isn't clouding his future. His old threat to kill Dialman made headlines when his sister was murdered. It won't take long for someone to put two and two together."

"Evan, how have you survived when you wear blinders?"

"What are you taking about?"

"Money. Who stands to gain and who loses?"

"Little McIntyre. I suppose it's winner take all."

"Like hell, she is...not with Thornton Thomas Towbridge in the picture. His family fidelity is a load of bull. He has one interest. Money.

"Ever been to his so-called horse farm with a stable full of nags that can barely make it around a pasture? It's over the county line."

"What farm? He lives here in town."

"Sure he does, a house in Old Town he inherited. Passed down through generations from late 1700s, within easy walking distance of McIntyre and Dialman's houses. Old home – old money. Have any idea what it costs to keep those places from falling down around your ears?"

"Never thought about it."

"Start. Then consider the upkeep on white fences, a pool the size of the one in Memorial Coliseum, cabin cruiser on the river, landing pad, stables, grand colonial mansion, almost as old as the townhouse, four smaller 'cottages,' huge pre-Derby parties with all the trimmings including State

Police for security guards, which is how I'm acquainted with the set-up out there. He inherited all right, but he had an older brother and younger sister in the picture back then, now both are dead.

"He managed to marry his niece off to Duncan Abbott, a nothing if there ever was one. Has them installed nice and cozy in one of the cottages. Along comes another niece with a healthy packet of her own. He suddenly goes sentimental. He can't spell the word."

I don't admit it to Curt, but when you look at his way, there are more questions than answers. Towbridge played me for a sucker. Took the bait. He knew what string to pull. I'd told him about the guys at the gym from the Bottoms.

"There's no way I can go to the courthouse and dig through old files without it getting back to TT. Don't suggest sending someone else, it wouldn't be the same."

"I had Jordan Ames in mind. It was obvious he was calling the shots as far as Clayton's security was concerned. He is Miss McIntyre's lawyer. He'd have a legitimate reason for checking old wills, deeds, and property tax records. You can give him the heads up on what to look for, the next time he is in town."

"You're right."

"Going to have to put Clayton's problem on the back burner. Miss McIntyre is first in line for your attention. I have to meet her."

"For what reason?"

"Your bad taste in women is a matter of record. I want to meet one who has you biting your nails."

"Twelve years ago in another life."

"Yeah, and the scars are still open. How did Towbridge find out about your name change?"

"Damn if I know. Mole in Maddy's network was my first conclusion."

"Have you told her?"

"Funny. I'll get the check. I don't have the day off."

"I'll call the coroner and have him keep an eye out for your carcass."

Chapter 14

Charity scrubbed behind the desk until her knuckles were raw, but the smell won't come out. I know I won't be able to work in this room sitting right over the awful odor. There is no help for it – the carpeting, must be replaced.

When the workmen take up the old carpeting they find Mr. Dialman's blood had soaked through the padding. Desper immediately calls Mr. Johnson at the police department, to come out and look.

Mr. Blade comes charging in, flinging orders like he owns the place. He, Desper, and Mr. Johnson have words outside, where I can't hear what they're saying. He is furious I'd call workmen to remove the carpeting, plus the hideous wallpaper in the reception parlor.

He can suck an egg.

I'm not stupid. I had Charity check with Maddy Sorals to get her recommendation, before I hired anyone.

As a way of an apology he came back later and helped us polish the beautiful parquet flooring, hidden under the carpeting. Afterwards, he and Desper reinstall the shelving while Charity and I arrange the furnishings. We work until nearly midnight.

He left, before we finished and returned with huge cornbeef sandwiches, crisp hash browns, a keg of beer, and what they called a derby pie, so rich it made my teeth sing.

We picnicked in the kitchen.

Evan Blade can be nice when he tries.

In the morning, I'm unpacking my books and refilling the boxes with law books when the door bell rings. Desper is mowing in the backyard and Charity is out shopping so I go to the door. I check through the window and open the door to Mr. Ames.

"Hello. I didn't expect you so soon. I don't have all the law books packed."

Why is it every time he arrives I look like a lost urchin wearing jeans and a t-shirt?

"Please come in."

"I didn't mean to disturb you."

"No..."

Charity runs up the hall, removing a large straw hat.

"Do we have coffee?"

"I'll make fresh. I got a pound cake."

She looks at Mr. Ames for agreement. He starts laughing.

"Is it stale?"

"No, Sir. Just got back from the grocery."

"What a shame. The first time I served my wife tea all I had was stale pound cake. She ate it and didn't say a word. It was the beginning of my favorite romance."

"Have you inspected Robert Dialman's house?"

"No. We've been busy with the renovations to this house. You say I own his house, yet it doesn't seem real to me."

"Then it's time you take a tour of your shotgun house."

"My what?"

"Come outside and look. If you stand on the street and fire a gun through the front door the bullet will travel through the house and out the backdoor."

"That is silly."

"Yes and no. The real reason houses were built one room attached to next extending back through the lot was to escape heavy property taxes. When it was built, the tax bill was assessed by the footage fronting on the street.

"Then if you were the builder you could get two and sometimes three on the same lot, which gave you a nice profit on your investment."

I look up at Mr. Ames. He is smiling at a memory.

"You know more about the history of Capital City than I do."

"Yes, Marcus McIntyre loved this small town that will never make a city. Its only excuse for existing was a ford across the river and its location in the middle of the state.

111

When I visited we'd take walks in the evening. He would point out the famous structures and tell us their history."

"Walking through history is more fun than reading about it."

"I have a vested interest in discovering who murdered Marcus McIntyre. He was the father I knew. My own died over the English Channel during World War II. My best memory of him is a photograph of a brash young flyer taken the day he got his wings."

"I'm sorry."

"Nothing for you to be sorry about. It happened a long time ago. Acres and acres of Europe are covered with Americans who didn't come home. I was luckier than many guys my age who lost a parent in that war. I had Marcus in my life.

"Blade is doing everything he can, to keep whoever is out there from hurting you. I don't agree with him. Not telling you the truth is protecting you. It may do the opposite and expose you to danger.

"Clayton intended to tell you what he knew about the past. Time ran out for him. Blade is working blind, putting the pieces together and he has the help of the state and city police. Clayton vows he is a good man who eventually will find the answers."

"I see."

"Petra. Do you mind if I call you by your first name?

"I called you that when I pushed you in a swing. You called me Jord. In a strange way I'm your much older brother through marriage and adoption."

"An older brother sounds nice, Jordan."

"Let's go inside. It won't do to let Charity's delicious coffee get cold.

"I'll tell you '*the rest of the story*.'"

~ ~ ~

The afternoon flies as Jordan tells me about the man who adopted me after my mother was murdered.

His step-father was a high profile city lawyer, who had lived his entire life in this brick home he willed to me.

Clients came from all walks of life. He was deeply respected by members of the community because he avoided politics and never took sides on the various issues which affected the city and its citizens.

Marcus McIntyre helped Ophelia Laurence, Mary's aunt operate an underground railroad for women and children whose lives were in danger long before any rumors of private endeavors in the area became known. Mary is going through her aunt's papers looking for anything that pertains to me. It's a tedious job that takes time.

Jordan was in the service when his mother died of cancer. When he returned for the funeral I didn't live in this house. Two years later when he was home on leave I was living here. Marcus told him I was the daughter of a friend he was keeping while the neighbor was out of town.

Elton Fightmaster informed him of Mr. McIntyre's death a few months later. As he was stationed in Alaska he didn't learn about the murder when it happened. His first marriage was in shambles. He'd vowed to himself, to become a lawyer once he retired from the military.

After Mr. Fightmaster sent Mr. Dialman to him to draw up his will he showed him a copy of my adoption papers. They were back dated to two years before his mother died. The date didn't make sense, but the papers had been signed, notarized, and filed with the Ono County Court.

Clayton explained to him his reasons and actions for hiding me when Mr. McIntyre was murdered. How I disappeared as if I didn't exist.

They tried a butcher paper method his wife, Connie, and Mary Laurence had used to solve a murder in Ono County. Like their wives, they'd acquired a lot of facts, which lead to more confusion than a solution.

I listen with every bone in my body. In a strange way, I feel like I'm back in school. My fingers itch to take notes.

From the first time I met him, I'd trusted Jordan Ames. Maybe it's the freckles below the Nordic eyes. It could be the lopsided grin. Maybe it was because anyone who takes to the sea respects rough waters. Somewhere I remember a man in uniform who pushed a lost child in a swing.

I like the idea of an older brother, who doesn't treat me like I'm a nitwit idiot.

I hold back, cautious. I don't tell him about the birth certificate Mrs. Emmens had given me when I left Valley View.

"I've told you everything we know."

"Petra, please be careful who you talk to and don't give Blade a hard time. I can't be here all the time. Clayton's recovery is going to take longer than he expected."

"I'm still trying to absorb what you've told me."

"I know. It's confusing. Are you up to taking a look across the street."

"Yes."

"You don't need to make immediate decisions. I know from experience, when a home is allowed to sit empty, little problems tend to become major ones. It took me three months to evict the bats and squirrels who'd taken up residence in my grandparents' attic."

I laugh at his story. I'd been avoiding even thinking about Mr. Dialman and his will.

"May Charity go with us? She and Desper have cared for this house for eight years. They'll be able to spot any immediate problems."

"Excellent idea. Don't worry, there won't be any ghosts. The City Police have reached the conclusion he wasn't shot in the house.

115

"Are you aware this area of Capital City suffered a major flood last December?"

"No one mentioned it. I haven't seen any flood damage."

"You won't from the outside. All these streets were the first residential homes to be cleaned after the waters went down. Many famous people in Kentucky history built their homes here, so it's a major tourist mecca. When the dogwoods and redbud trees are in bloom in the spring, they flock here after visiting the Capitol. It's important to the city's economy for it to look its best."

"I see."

"I suspect the high brick walls around gardens are a private flood wall system the early settlers installed for protection from the river."

"Makes sense. The walls are easy to climb. I did it last week."

"And?"

"Mr. Blade didn't want the police to see me. I got tired of waiting on the floorboard of his truck. So I came in the back way over the fence. From the way he carried on you'd of thought I'd committed one of the original sins."

"Petra, I believe we can tackle an empty house with impunity. I have a key."

~ ~ ~

He was wrong.

The minute we entered I knew I'd been in this house. The stairs I'd expected, when I first arrived at Mr. McIntyre's were here, to the side of a long hall leading to the back of the house.

With each step I'm afraid of what I'll find, though the rooms are void of furniture, except for a large breakfront in what must have been the dining room. There are water stains up about my waist in the rooms and paper is peeling from the walls.

Desper explains the neighbors came in and helped the homeowners move their furniture up to the second floor, to escape the flood waters. Mr. Dialman's had never been moved back.

The kitchen is plain and surprisingly clean. A dainty cup sits on the counter with dregs of tea in the bottom. The kettle still has water in it. A rumble from the basement proves to be a little dehydrator, draining into a laundry sink. A small effort to dry out the house.

"Miss Petra, you'd best get bigger units in here to dry the plaster, before it all ruins."

"Thanks, Desper. Can you see to it for me?"

"Yes, several places in town are well stocked now as the major cleanup is finished. Mr. Dialman must never have asked for help.

"That is sad. He was a knowing man."

The rooms upstairs are a different story.

At the head of the stairs is a small bedroom, which was obviously a child's room. Now, it holds a lovely Duncan Phyffe dining table and matching chairs. Against one wall is a Queen Anne silver chest. Linens, dishes, and glassware are piled around the room and on the little canopied bed.

Jordan, Charity, and Desper stand back letting me explore. I don't mention the familiar feeling I got when I opened the door to the little bedroom.

A bathroom-dressing room is between two large bedrooms. One facing my house is feminine and comfortable, even with twin sofas, side tables, and chairs stacked against one wall. I sit down on a stool before a dresser with triple mirrors. Nothing remains of the child I know, who had played here laughing at her multiple images.

I step back when I open the door to Mr. Dialman's suite. It has been ransacked. Drawers hang open, papers littered the floor, books are strewn around, lying open with their spines cracked, coverings pulled from the bed, and his clothes are scattered across the floor.

"Don't touch anything. You must call the police. This was done after they finished their investigation. There no mention of it in their report.

"Charity, you and Petra go across the street. I'll be over in a minute."

He pulls the door closed. Looks at his watch and says, "Damn.

"Desper, go arrange for the dehydrators and while you're up town, get new locks. Hurry, it's getting near closing time. The burglar has Dialman's keys. They weren't listed in his effects file."

"Mr. Ames, Mr. Dialman had a key to Miss McIntyre's house. He checked on it when we were working elsewhere."

"Get locks for both houses. Once the police leave, we're going to be busy. Where is Blade?"

"I don't know. We were up late last night polishing the floors."

"Petra, call the police and report the break-in.

"Charity, call Maddy Sorals. She'll locate Blade. Tell her I need him as soon as possible."

Chapter 15

Jordan left. I hate to see him leave, but he has an appointment with the judge at the court house before it closes.

The police arrive and Desper meets them at Mr. Dialman's house. Charity and I stay in the parlor watching from the front window. There is nothing to see. When questioned, we can't tell them if anything was taken because it was our first time to enter the house.

Jordan returns as they're leaving. We hadn't mentioned he was with us in the house. He talks to Mr. Johnson as my lawyer, questioning him more than he answers questions.

I fight a case of the giggles. It's smooth. Poor Mr. Johnson. He unconsciously recognizes the aura of command Jordan exudes, behind the freckles, and responds without knowing he'd done so.

We learn from Mr. Johnson, a man by the name of Duncan Abbott had claimed Mr. Dialman's body, as next of kin and the funeral will be Tuesday afternoon at Holy Cross Episcopal Church. He is to be buried next to his wife, in the family cemetery on TT Towbridge's farm.

I met a Mr. Abbott the day Mr. Blade...Evan, took me to lunch at Serafini. I didn't like him.

When Mr. Johnson was leaving, he tells us a vacant house invites break-ins. People in town are beginning, to have someone 'baby-sit' the house, until after a funeral since there had been a rash of break-ins when bunglers knew the family was elsewhere.

"Desper, would it be an inconvenient for you and Charity to move into the Dialman house?"

"What do you have in mind, Sir?"

"Several reasons. I broached notice of Miss McIntyre's inheritance to Judge Roach. I filed in Ono County, so it was a matter of legal record, before I made the filing here in Ridgeway County. A simple matter of legal precautions to prevent countersuits by other relatives, besides there is a little house in Clydesville that belonged to Mr. Dialman's grandmother. It is rented to Ralph Parker and his family.

"Judge Roach let slip that several distant family members had been asking about probate status. Whoever entered Dialman's house was looking for some thing...probably his will.

"Someone inhabiting the property also establishes claim if anyone files a countersuit. All is legal beagle maneuvering. The important thing is Petra's safety. I'm convinced, this is a killer who intends to eliminate anyone who stands in his way.

"The front bedroom of the Dialman house looks directly across into the bedroom Petra is using. If you used a pair of binoculars, it will be possible to keep an eye on this house."

Desper hesitates and looks at Charity. She slowly nods her head.

"Its been crowded at my parent's place since the flood. We lost our trailer. The neighbors will kick up a fuss."

His face is sad. I butt in blazing. What he was implying is ugly.

"In what way?"

"Miss Petra, we aren't the right color for this neighborhood."

"Segregation ended ages ago."

"It did according to the law, not in people's minds."

"Petra, he is correct. It's difficult to combat and may not cease for many years to come."

He grins the most sneaky, crafty grin I've ever seen.

"I have an idea. We'll use their perceptions to our advantage."

"How?"

"Desper, do you still have the insurance money you received for your trailer?"

"It isn't much after the loan was paid off. Got the check last week. Deposited in a bank money market account."

"Good man. What I want you to do is pack some suitcases and move into Dialman's house. Someone must be

122

on the premises to oversee the necessary flood damage repairs."

"Yes, Sir. I understand about seeing to the repairs, but why were you asking about our insurance money? We've been saving, looking for a place we can afford. Prices have gone up since the flood.

"There are rumors the entire Bottoms is going to be leveled to make way for a federal revitalization project. My parents are worried they'll lose their home and it's up a ways on Reservation Hill."

"I suspected as much when I drove through the area and saw bulldozers sitting around on trucks. I saw it happen when I was a boy when the dam was built in Ono County. Fine people lost farms which had been in their family from land grants passed out for service in the Revolutionary War.

"Petra, you told me last week you didn't want Dialman's house. Are you still of the same mind?"

"Billy Bejaysus, yes. I told you. I've got enough problems with this house, which I can't afford. Much less two."

"Good. Dialman was also entitled to flood damage insurance to cover the repairs. If he hadn't filed a claim for it, then I'll file in your name."

The best lawyers can get long winded. I'm getting impatient with him for beating around the bush and get sarcastic.

"Thank you, Mr. Ames. Will you be sending me a bill for the extra services?"

"No, Miss McIntyre. The court covers those problems with a percentage of the estate going to the executor. Can't afford to work for free. A military pension doesn't go that far."

He paid me back in kind. We both laughed with complete understanding.

Chapter 16

Jordan and I agreed. He'd call his wife to tell her not to expect him back until morning. He will spend the night here to share our plans and help change the locks.

Evan Blade and Whoof came in the back door, as Charity was pulling a pork roast from the oven. The man has a positive instinct for knowing when she is fixing a big meal.

While Jordan and I discussed his spur of the moment idea, she'd managed to pull together a delicious supper of scalloped potatoes, green beans with grilled pineapple and hot rolls.

While we eat, Jordan describes his plan for the Dialman house. It's so simple – I'm ashamed I hadn't thought of it myself. Larger in scope, though much like the deal we worked out for the law books.

I'd never asked about the lives Desper and Charity were living. I'd accepted their help without question and depended on them in the same manner as masters had their of slaves, for my comfort and well being.

125

Some detective I'll make when I don't pay attention to small details of my own home. Jordan had done the homework I'd ignored when I walked Whoof around the neighborhood.

I had noticed I never saw children playing in the quiet streets. It never dawned on me, that behind those closed doors and curtained windows lived people who are getting along in years like Mr. Dialman.

Jordan explains it to Charity and Desper. Evan looks puzzled as if anyone should know so basic a fact. I wink at him and he catches my eye. Still, he is surprised by the overt audacity of our method of defeating local prejudice.

Desper and Charity are established in the neighborhood, because of their work for Clayton. People are accustomed to seeing them coming and going. Out of kindness, over the years, they'd helped my neighbors by carrying in a heavy bag of groceries, moving furniture during the flood, plowing up a garden, and shoveling walks after snow storms.

They'll give me a security payment of one hundred dollars on the Dialman house. Jordan will draw up a land contract for the transaction, which states when the house is repaired, thus liveable, I will deed it to them or remain their mortgage holder, whichever method is agreeable to both parties at the time of conveyance.

They'll continue to help me maintain my home, for which they both will receive a partial payment, with the remainder to be credited against the purchase price.

He'll see the transaction is a matter of record at the court house. He reasons, by the time all matters are settled and the repairs completed, the residents won't notice the color of their skin.

Jordan instructs Evan to take me to the different utility offices to change their accounts to my name, for both houses. Another item I'd missed, though I had noticed the electric bill was much lower this month. The high bills were from when dehumidifiers were running night and day, to dry out the house after the flood.

The care they gave this place is evidence of their skills, because I hadn't been aware of water damage to the premises.

The good sisters would be appalled by my blindness. I'd been oblivious, like the spoiled brat Evan calls me.

~ ~ ~

Whoof and I slept late after a long evening of changing locks and snacks of left overs. Everyone has gone by the time we go down stairs to the kitchen.

I take time to read the notes scattered on the counter before fixing Whoof's lead for his walk. Four blocks over is a derelict old stable he likes to investigate and use to do his business. It's a brisk walk, pulled by a dog who weighs more than I do.

We pass a large man who nods and lifts his hat. Whoof pauses for a brief pet before plunging on to his chosen destination.

When we come back at a sedate pace the man is leaning against the light post on the corner, reading a newspaper. Whoof again stops for a pet. He knows the man and doesn't consider him a threat.

"Morning ma'am. Best time for a walk before it get's too hot."

He hands me the newspaper.

"This is yours. I borrowed it to catch up on the doings in town."

"Do I know you? I've seen you before."

"Yes, ma'am. Keepin' an eye out while Desper is movin'. Nice thin' you did for him and his misses. They is fine people."

"Keeping an eye on me?"

"Yes, ma'am. Mr. Clayton would boil me in oil if anythin' happen to you on his watch."

I look up at him. Clayton is tall. This man is huge, with bulging muscles in his shoulders and arms that strain his shirt. He is closer to Evan's age than Clayton's. He could easily pick my guardian up and throw him across the street.

"If you say so."

His craggy face lights with a smile of a gentle giant.

"Oh, I do ma'am, I've known him a long time. He and Evan Blade too. They can be hard men to deal with when they're crossed.

"Have a good day, ma'am."

~ ~ ~

128

Whoof nudges his food bowl across the floor against my feet to get my attention. I open a can of wet food and dump it in the clean dish. For a dog who belongs to a man, he is fastidious about his food. The dish must be clean.

I scramble eggs and make tea, while thinking I'm going to have to get Charity to teach me to cook. I've watched her toast the beans for coffee. When I tried it, they were a scorched failure.

I'm turning the paper to the classifieds to see what kind of jobs are being offered when my eye catches a small paragraph buried at the bottom of a page in the middle of the paper.

> *Mrs. Florence Emmens, 75, retired director of The Valley View Children's Home was shot from outside her home in Piketon while she was reading by a window.*

Matron has been murdered. My memories of her aren't pleasant. She was a harsh, brutal woman who didn't tolerate crying or whining. I hated her when she slapped me after I fell down the stairs…no, no.

I was pushed!

Bad Man pushed me down the stairs yelling for Matron.

I was lying on the floor, my leg broken and crying. She slapped me and then ran up the stairs, leaving me in pain. They screamed at each other. I couldn't see his face. He didn't have his pants on.

I wore a cast on my leg that thumped when I walked. The man was gone. I never saw him again. I knew when he was present. My door was locked.

The older girls told me I was lucky to be a nigger. He didn't like me.

I stare out the window above the sink, at the tall white daisies dancing in the sun. The ugly memory wipes out all the glow from last night.

How old I was, maybe six or seven. I'd accepted what I'd been told…I fell when I didn't. I was pushed. The pain destroyed my memory of the real events.

This morning I'd watched out the window of my room as Desper and Charity carried their bags into their new home. I ignored an ache of despair. A feeling something bad was going to happen to them. I felt abandoned.

I want to escape the oppressive emptiness of the house, yet I have no where to go.

I'm uncomfortable with Jordan's idea of them watching from the upstairs window. It's like I'm living in a fish bowl.

I run upstairs to get my lucky sailor's hat one of the cadets had given me when I first learned to sail. The river is as close as I can get to the open sea where I'm free.

~ ~ ~

Whoof doesn't leave my side even when I remove his lead. The yard below the alley goes down to old stone steps leading across a flood plain. We walk around a rectangle of an old vegetable garden. Tangled in the weeds I see a few volunteer tomato plants.

A stone path goes down to a dock on the river. The man I met this morning is sitting there fishing.

"Hello. Catching anything?"

"No, ma'am. Fish don't bite much when weather is this hot. Wouldn't want to eat 'em. Taste like mud."

"We met this morning."

"No, ma'am. He was my brother, Anvil. I'm Wedge Forge, we is twins."

"Strange names."

"Oh no, ma'am. They is fittin'. Ancestor come over the mountains. He didn't have no last name, so bein' a blacksmith he named himself for his trade."

Mr. Forge has the same gentle smile as his brother.

"Best we figure, he was with one of those German outfits the British brought over during the Revolution. Run off, most likely, and got his-self attached to our side. Back when they used horses, an Army always had work for a blacksmith. Got a grant and took up farming in Ovendecker Bottom, down in what is now Ono County. It was Virginia back then.

"When we come along, the farm was gone under the lake and black smithin' was almost a thing of the past. Our daddy declared he'd keep the memory in the family and named us for his trade.

"Ma'am, you shouldn't be down here listenin' to me jawin' about water gone over the milldam."

"Whoof needed a run. Refuses to leave me. I have to take him."

"Blade put him to guarding you. He won't go until he is released. Don't like the river."

I can feel Whoof panting behind me. If I had a bathing suit I wouldn't mind taking a swim, even if the water is muddy.

"How do I get him to take a run on his own?"

"Don't know. Evan has a secret command."

"May I join you? My name is Petra McIntyre."

"Know who you are, ma'am."

"It's cool down here."

"Shouldn't cause no harm. It's your dock we're a sittin' on."

"This dock belongs to me?"

"Sure does. Good building. Came through the floor in tip top shape. Good place to tie up a little runabout. Should be no bigger. Rivers are funny things. Dry spell hits and even with the locks there are places you can walk across and not get your feet wet. For fishing, get yourself a flat bottom johnboat. You won't have trouble getting it out on the water. Easy to haul out in winter."

"I love being on water."

"Nothing moving this afternoon.

"Brother didn't see you come this way or he'd be a bellerin'. Do you fish?"

"No. I've collected oysters. Never fished. When you're handling the sails you're too busy to stop and catch fish."

"Don't have but one pole. Here give it a try."

He baits the hook and shows me how to throw it out in the water. I let the current carry the bobber down stream then wind the line on the reel to pull it back. Part of the worm is gone, but I throw it again.

It's peaceful. I can hear grasshoppers rubbing their wings and a few sleepy bird calls. The air around us has a heavy smell that makes you to want to lean back against a post and take a nap.

"You remind me of a paintin' by Norman Rockwell. Boy sittin' on a post by a stream with a dog watchin' his every move."

"Mr. Forge, are you making fun of me because I haven't caught a fish?"

"No ma'am. Fishin' this time of day ain't for catchin'. It's for cogitatin'."

"For cogitating?"

"Sure. I've been sitting here tryin' to think up a way to ask you about some business."

"Business?"

"See..."

He holds out his hands with the thumbs touching and then points up one side with his index finger.

"We have a little marina on Tuckingham Lake. We don't take no rowdies, just folks who enjoy fishin' and swimmin' in quiet peace. A row of slips moored on our side of the cove. Another row on this side. They're anchored on your land."

"My land?"

"Yes, Mr. Dialman owned the farm across from us. Now it's yours. Have to come across one of his hayfields to get down to the water. On our side is a steep cliff. It's a good spot, plenty deep. We want to keep it. That is if you don't mind."

"Why should I mind? It's the first I've heard about a farm."

He jumps up with surprising agility for a man his size and grabs my pole.

"Give me that, girl. You've got a bite!"

It wasn't much of a fish. Maybe a foot long. Mr. Forge took it off the hook and threw it back in the water.

I want to show it off.

I caught a fish!

He is telling me about a house trailer, mounted on pontoons his brother found. They want to spruce it up as a snack bar and small grocery, to join the two rows of slips together, when we hear the distinct rumble of powerful diesel engines roaring like a Greyhound Bus. They're slightly out of sync, making a *rump bump-bump* sound.

A sleek blue and white Fairlane custom cabin cruiser, moving very slow, comes around a bend in the river. I'd seen several like it moored at the marina on the bay. Those twin 6-71 Detroits with super and turbo chargers are too big for this river. It's an ocean going boat, built to withstand high seas in a gale.

"Has more money than he has sense. Boat is TT Towbridge's baby, *Dreamer.* He is the Lieutenant Governor. Showin' off for some foreign dignitaries."

"There is a man in the stern, watching us through binoculars."

"I see him. That'd be Duncan Abbott. Doesn't go anywhere without him followin' behind. Towbridge is in the wheel house. He always runs the show."

"Does he always run just above idle?"

"Have too. Since the flood it's easy to hit a sawyer floatin' under the water, even in the middle. Can take out the bottom in nothin' flat."

"Hard on those big engines. Juan Torres would call him a fool."

"Funny, I don't see anyone else on her. Why is he out here in the middle of the week, when there isn't anyone around to impress?

"Missy, you continue fiddlin' with the hook. Make 'em think you're a boy. Then get up casual like, keepin' your head turned. Take Whoof and head back up the hill.

"Don't be scared. I'm goin' to start whistlin'. Anvil'll meet you."

Chapter 17

Meet Ames at Turleys for breakfast before he starts back to Ono County. A different man from the friendly big-brother of the previous night. Doesn't waste time with social amenities. He comes straight to the point.

Small yellow legal pad's beside his coffee cup, which he uses for notes in a code I can't read upside down or otherwise.

"Clayton is a long time friend. We were in the same class up to the seventh grade. Never saw him again until I returned to Ono County, after I retired from the Coast Guard.

"Dr. Flanders says the bullet he took, tore him up inside. The doctor here did an excellent job of repair and saved his life. His recovery is going to be much slower than anticipated due both to his age and the extent of the damage. He is aware of this and told me he'd turned everything over to you.

"He sent you this."

Ames hands me a bank envelope. I break the seal. It's stuffed with hundred dollar bills. More cash money than I've ever seen at one time, in one place.

"His orders are to keep the dollars, pounds and franks he gave you and return by me the other miscellaneous currency."

"What did he do, rob a bank?"

"Don't ask me. I'm the delivery boy."

"What else did he have to say?"

"His exact words were, 'You're to find the son-of-a-bitch who killed McIntyre. Then take down the responsible party or parties for putting Petra's life on the line, no matter how big the toes you step on in the process.'"

"And?"

"I concur. Marcus McIntyre was my step-father. He made my mother very happy. He was a good man who once told me he'd never defended an innocent person. I have his files in the trunk of my car and will go through them. I doubt I'll find anything after the break-in."

"Could the killer and the second-story man be two different people?"

"It's possible, but not probable. The break-ins occurred after the murders, as if he was searching for something...papers specifically or files. Nothing of any value was taken. With both it was their papers. Indication is it was a hurried job as no effort was made to conceal the search."

"Good morning, gentleman."

Lieutenant Colton's standing by our booth. Smoky the Bear hat tops his full uniform. Damn him he came in the backdoor. Start to scoot over in the booth. He stops me.

"Can't stay. Have a class in ten minutes. Thought you might want to know before it gets out on the wires. A Mrs. Florence Emmens, in Mason County, was killed with the same type bullet as Dialman. She was the former director of the Valley View Children's Home."

He drops the bomb and leaves before I can ask a question.

"That's were Clayton stashed Petra after McIntyre was murdered."

"What did he mean when he said 'same type of bullet'?"

Explain to Ames how McIntyre, Dialman, and Clayton were shot with bullets, which were cross-hatched before they were loaded in the weapon.

"In the movies you'll sometimes see the villain cut the nose off bullets. In the trade, those are called dumb-dumbs. Make a good size hole going in and one hell of a hole coming out.

"This guy's an amateur, according to Curt. He used a nailfile. Another thing we know, he was close to the victim with the exception of Clayton. So he's someone they knew.

"Then there's Mrs. Dialman's death, different method. Both she and her husband were beaten before they were killed."

"Why were they killed? They were prominent citizens in the community? Another strange thing, the Dialman's were removed from where they were killed. Marcus and Clayton were left where they were shot."

"Ames, Clayton told me he dropped immediately, rolled, and hid in the bushes. Ever see the scar he has running down from his left ear? He got it in Korea, hid under bodies until some Turks pulled him out. Been there too many times to stick around waiting to give a shooter a chance at a second shot."

"Clayton was unexpected. He came by water. Maybe the killer was leaving by the same route and shot Clayton to eliminate a witness to his presence. Told me he'd forgotten Petra's graduation.

"We were dealing with some Vegas hoods who broke in Mary's house. He was having supper with her when he remembered. Left her grilling steaks and high tailed it up here, still towing his cruiser. They'd planed to relax on the lake the next day. Didn't take time to unhook. Since he had the boat he made use of it.

"No one knew Clayton was involved, with the exception of the latest victim, Mrs. Emmens. I'll ask him when I see him."

Ames scribbles more notes on his pad. Then runs his pen down the page. I count with him.

"Four people murdered who had a connection to Petra. Their deaths leave TT Towbridge. He's her blood uncle. He demanded I find his sister's killer. Told him I'd look into it. Gave me a file of items he had collected over the years.

"Is he behind the killings and using me for a cover or is he in line to become the next victim?"

"What do you know about the man?"

"TT? Politician who loves money, prestige, and power. Not necessarily in the same order. Curt says he needs money. Told me to go looking in hall of records. A chore best accomplished with a lock pick, in the dark of the moon."

"Then we'll do it tonight."

"We? You can't. You're an officer of the court."

"Evan, I'll pick you up at your place after dark. We have the same client. If Towbridge isn't the next candidate for execution, then she is."

~ ~ ~

If Ames hadn't become a lawyer, he'd made one of the top second-story men in the business. Thought I was good with a lock pick. He was through the basement door of the court house faster than who flung the chunk.

Knew the drill, dark car, dark clothes, soft soled shoes, and surgical gloves. They fit like a second skin.

141

Musty, stale air clogs my nose. County hasn't finished drying out the nether regions from the flood. Ames carries a pen light in his teeth. Its feeble beam get us to the stairs without banging our shins and up to the lobby.

We stay in the shadows with our backs to the wall. Careful to side step to the Clerk's office.

"Watch those big cables on the floor. They're doing crude computer files. At the rate they're going, it will be the next century before they're finished. I'll take the probate court records. You tackle property transfers. Tax records are upstairs in the Sheriff's office."

We go to work. Clara Dialman died in June of 1964. When I find her will, I whistle. She'd left everything to her husband, including her one-third share of all Towbridge holdings. Marcus McIntyre had prepared the will and served as executor of her estate. Her estate had been finalized and released from the probate court on December 7, 1964. He was killed on December 8th.

Bet a monkey's uncle December 7th, besides being the day the Japs bombed Pearl Harbor, was the first Monday of the month, Court Day. Have a nasty feeling Clara Dialman signed Marcus McIntyre's death warrant.

Come near shooting through the ceiling when Ames speaks.

"Got some dimes?"

"Dimes?"

"Xerox machine takes dimes. I'm fresh out."

Fish in my pocket and come up with six.

"Copy this while you're at it. We'll get out of here. Feel like someone's walking on my grave."

~ ~ ~

Go back to my place to change clothes. His boots are a marvel.

"Where did you get those?"

"Alaska. Intuits make them – made of walrus hide and wear like iron. Hot in the summer, but perfect for long nights on a winter sea. Keep you're feet warm and dry."

"Get up and help me move my bed."

"Why?"

"You said Clayton wanted the foreign currency."

We move the bed and remove the tiles in the corner. Under them's a heavy wood lid. Under it a large steel safe, incased in concrete. Open the safe and take out the briefcase Clayton had given me.

Been debating with myself since Ames told me about the currency Clayton wanted returned. Have to trust someone with the mess. Maybe Ames can keep me out of prison.

Put the case on my desk and open it. When he sees the lettuce, he draws in a sharp breathe.

"Is that real?"

"I guess."

143

"Evan, there is close to fifty thousand dollars there. Those odd looking bills are Swiss Bank notes, redeemable in gold. I'm not up on the current rates of exchange."

Get a plain brown envelope and stuff it with the bills. Leaving what Clayton had instructed me to keep. He might need it in the future.

"The money isn't what's driving me crazy. Do you have time to take a look at some papers?"

"Sure."

Hand him the damn things. Grit my teeth to keep from shaking. Then wait while he reads each page, mentally biting my nails.

"So, everything is in order. You're on extended leave from military duties, due to an injury. What is the problem?"

"They're forgeries."

"If they are, it's the slickest job I've ever seen."

"Drafted. Served two tours and part of a third when I was injured in 'Nam. Given a medical discharge under another name. Knew nothing about those damn things until I opened the briefcase he gave me, the night you took Clayton home. Don't want to spend the rest of my life in Leavenworth for fraud."

"My learned legal advice is – put this back in your safe and keep it on ice. Tackle Clayton after we get current business settled. He isn't going anywhere with a hole in his gut and Mary's baby on the way. He holds the keys.

"Pardon me for asking, but how did you get your nose broken?"

"Some guys didn't like the old one. They gave me a new one."

"In other words, it's none of my business."

~ ~ ~

Call Pat Bihn. He let us in the back door. It's after last call, but we aren't drinking.

Pat grins as he put two steaming Turkey Manhattans and salads on the table with iced tea.

"If anyone asks, you've been here playing poker all evening?"

"Thanks, but why would anyone ask?"

"Haven't you heard?"

"Heard what?"

"It came over my scanner, about a half-hour ago. Some kids broke in the court house. Got into the Sheriff's records to destroy their rap sheets. Billy Ray cornered them. They've been swearing they followed two guys into the building.

"An old drunk is declaring he saw two guys from his jail cell window come out the courthouse's back door and drive away.

"Johnson is out combing the streets. Looking for two guys in dark clothes driving a dark car."

"Pat, do our white shirts look like dark clothes? As you said, we've been here all evening, playing poker. Billy Ray will enjoy it when you tell him I dropped a bundle to a country lawyer."

"'*Oh, the tangled web we weave when first we practice to deceive.*'"

"That's one Shakespeare quote I've never heard from Lon Chambers."

"Isn't from the bard, but a close proximity. Sir Walter Scott. Let's trade information and see if we fill in some blanks."

I'd visited the Bureau of Vital Statistics. There was no record of the birth of a Vivian Phillips Dialman as shown on her hospital issued birth certificate. Called on TT.

He told me she was born in New York. Dialman and his sister had an RH factor problem. Her previous pregnancies had ended in miscarriages or still births. When she became pregnant with Petra they weren't taking any chances. She went to New York and stayed near a hospital where they were equipped to do an immediate blood exchange, if the baby was born what he called 'a blue baby.' She came home with Vivian, a healthy child. The entire family was delighted. His mother got to hold her second grandchild before she died.

Ames frowns. He thinks Dialman's birth certificate is phoney. Neither of us can come up with an answer as to why the subterfuge.

His previous research to identify estate assets indicate Dialman had left Petra comfortable, for the rest of her life, if she is careful.

There are stocks, mostly Kentucky Utilities Preferred. Besides the house and furnishings, the farm above Tuckingham Lake, his grandmother's little house in Clydesville, and a surprise, he owned the stable the preservationists are fighting over. Plus three buildings, in downtown Capital City, rented to a number of tenants.

There is no question she'll inherit, because he'd named her as Petra Isolta McIntyre and identified her as the adopted daughter of Marcus Laurence McIntyre.

The zinger is Clara Dialman's will, which I'd found. It left Towbridge hanging by his short hairs. He has two nieces, who together, own more of his parents' estate than he does.

Curt told me the entire mess was about money. Now I believe him.

Chapter 18

Brat's giving me the silent treatment sitting over there staring out the window like she has never seen green fields. Someone cut hay today and the smell floats in the window. Perfect weather for racing.

Been looking forward to seeing USA midgets race on a short dirt track for months. Jim Young told me Renee Anderson had talked Elroy Harris and Lon Chambers into building her a midget car. She'll get her pigtails trimmed, going up against professional drivers.

She's his albatross hanging around his neck like Pi's mine. Carl Anderson's granddaughter. Jim owes him, like I owe Clayton.

Of all the times for Anvil's wife to have her baby and an owner to bring a big houseboat to the marina. They had to go back to the lake, leaving me stuck with Pi, and no where to keep her out of trouble.

When I got to the house, where was she? Safe…reading a book in her room with all the doors locked? No. She was down on the dock…alone…fishing.

Raised hell when I hauled her ass back to the house by the seat of her pants. Told her to change clothes as she was going racing with me. Gave me some stupid song and dance about wanting to watch a silly TV program.

When Wedge told me about TT coming down the river and watching her through binoculars, I came near turning her over my knee and giving her the paddling she'd earned. Whoof is normally with her. Today I had to take him to get his rabies shot and have him flea-dipped.

How in the hell do Clayton and Ames expect me to keep her alive, when she is bound and determined to do the exact opposite of what I tell her?

~ ~ ~

Evan shoves me through the crowd like I'm a grocery cart.

Roar, zip. Roar, zip.

It sounds like every male in the parking lot is gunning his engine as high as he can, to see who can blow it out first. One clamor of thunder after another. The cacophony is like I'm standing it the middle of the Pennsylvania Turnpike, and cars without mufflers are whirling past me.

I put my hands over my ears. How can he stand this noise? It's making my head pound. I can't think.

We pass a building, a clod of mud hits me in the face almost knocking me down. He has the unmitigated gall to laugh as he cleans my face, like I'm a little kid who has been eating cotton candy.

When we reach the end of a tall fence, he walks up to a group of men and pushes me in front of him.

"Behave. These guys are friends of mine."

It's easy to see they have no interest in me. They're busy watching the cars run circles around the track. The cars slow down, dive over the edge and disappear behind a wall. The silence is welcoming to my weary ears.

One man turns as we approach. He looks like a pirate. I mean a real one, with a patch over one eye. He takes off his dust covered baseball cap.

"See you made it, Evan. Find a baby sitter for the brat?"

I stomp his toes as he pinches my shoulder.

"Who is your lady friend?"

"Jim Young, may I present 'the brat', Pi McIntyre."

"Ma'am, please forgive his big mouth. He has never been known to keep it shut. I'm Isaiah Young, he is my stupidest brother, Jim."

Isaiah Young has wolf eyes like Clayton. They change color.

"How many do you have?"

He holds up his hand and starts counting. His fingers are long and sculptured.

"Best I can figure, there are seven."

A big man lifts an eyebrow, halved by a deep scar which makes it wobble in a funny way.

"Always knew you couldn't count. We're a baseball team. Isaiah plays left field.

"Miss McIntyre, I'm pleased to meet you. I'm Matt Young."

The pirate gives his brothers a dirty look. Nods to me, slips around the fence, and walks across the track to the center, beating his cap against his leg.

"Jim is a tad nervous at the moment. He has a new car on the track, with an inexperienced driver. He doesn't want the paint job scratched before it has had a chance to dry."

While he is talking, more cars come out on the track and start roaring. I grab my ears.

A small elderly man takes my arm.

"Evan, didn't you tell your lady friend what to expect? Lon, take him down in the pits. Find some ear muffs for the lady. I'm Elroy Harris."

"I will when you introduce me."

"Pie, like good eatin'?"

"No, it's Pi like the circumference of a circle."

"I see. Miss Pi McIntyre, may I present, Lon Chambers. Well, go on, find her some muffs."

"Pleased to meet you, ma'am. Don't let him start telling you jokes while we work."

"She can't hear 'em no how in all this noise. Come with me. I'll get you the best seat in the house."

He escorts me down to the end of the row of bleachers, made out of boards laid on concrete blocks. He evicts some guys who are sitting on the front row with his white cane and sits me in their place, putting the cane on the bench behind us.

"Saving for the boys. Ole cane has more than one use. If a local yokel blocks your view, I'll poke him out of the way. This is the fourth turn, best seat in the house."

"How would you know?"

A small driver much the same size of a jockey is standing by my elbow.

"Don't need your sass. How'd she run?"

"Told Lon to adjust air in the tires on the right side. The bank is off a couple of degrees.

"Would you like to go to the restroom before the opening ceremonies?"

"Would I?"

Evan comes up behind the driver.

"Dragon lady won't let her in dressed like a sailor. She'll think she's a boy."

The driver pulls off the helmet exposing a mass of flaming red curls escaping from pigtails.

"No sweat, we settled that argument earlier. I'm Renee Anderson. Driving for Young Racing. It's Jim's first time to have a car in a USAC race."

"Renee, I'm Petra McIntyre. Pi to my friends.

"Where is the head? Haven't been since we left Capital City."

"In Evan's truck?"

"Yes."

"Come on. Dummy doesn't know the meaning of pit stop. That 4x4 High-Rider lumbers like a tank on a corduroy road. Hell on the ole bladder."

"Ever been to a big-time dirt track race?"

"Cars, no. Horses, yes."

"Where?"

"Maryland. Pimlico."

"Home of the Preakness?"

"Yes, it rained up until race time, more mud than dirt. Seattle Slew won."

"You must tell Elroy. He loves race horses. Still helps John Henry Burton exercise the yearlings. He is a dear."

By the time we get back to our seats, I know Jim Young builds racing engines. Isaiah is both an artist and has a Nashville recording contract. Matt played football for the Minnesota Vikings and owns the Capital City radio and TV station. Elroy and Lon are mechanics who make moonshine on the side. Elroy can't see and Lon can't hear.

Renee keeps talking a mile-a-minute. She has a nonchalant attitude she uses to hide a tremendous case of nerves.

"Renee, what is USAC?"

"I'm sorry. Evan didn't tell you a thing did he? USAC stands for United States Automobile Club. They're the guys that run the Indianapolis 500."

"Renee, stop talking and come on. We don't have all night."

Two men – twins like Anvil and Wedge have joined the group. One has a camera hanging around his neck. He takes Renee by the arm and drags her toward the middle of the racecourse. He is carrying a gun.

"The rude one is my brother, Abel. He has a one track mind. I'm Kane Young."

"I'm pleased to meet you, Mr. Young. I'm Pi McIntyre. I came with Evan Blade."

"Better use Kane. It can get confusing. I see you've met my brothers. You two, I have a message from Jim and I quote: 'To get the free passes for this crowd, he promised the owners you'd work tonight.'

"They're waiting for you at the grandstand."

~ ~ ~

Sultry heat presses down on the stands. The cars are pushed out on the track. Kane Young hands me a pair of binoculars and points down the rows to a brilliant blue car with a large "C" painted on the side. A nine is nestled inside the curves. Renee is standing beside it with her hair flying in the wind. She is arguing with Jim Young.

Behind me someone comments, "He is telling her to lay back and run a safe race. She is telling him she is racing to win."

"Ladies and gentlemen. Tonight we are proud to have a special treat for the first time here at Richmond Speedway.

"Give a big round of applause to the racing teams of USAC Midget Sprint Cars, a division of the famous Thunder and Lightening group. You saw a number of these same drivers race on Memorial Day in the 500. Let 'em know you want them to come back.

"Special visitors aren't the end of historic events. Young Racing has returned to our track to show the out-of-town-owners what a local racing team can field. Jim has managed to snare the prettiest driver I've ever seen on any track. He also brought along his own cheering section.

"His brother, Matt has agreed to call the race, just like he does in Minnesota for the Vikings.

"Please stand. Isaiah Young will lead us in singing the National Anthem."

The lights come on, focus on a tall flag pole in the center of the field. Men in full uniform from all branches of the armed services are holding the flag. A drum roll precedes the music as they attach the ropes. Isaiah's clear tenor begins to soar above the crowd, then everyone joins him as the flag ascends the pole. It reaches the top as the last notes die and flies free in the wind.

"Let's go racing" is drowned in the cheering.

Elroy explains, between bursts of noise, about qualifying times and heat races to allow drivers to participate in the main feature of 200 laps.

The cars look like kiddy cars as they bounce around the third of a mile track. Elroy tells me to watch the front of the cars, as they come into turn four, so close to us I can see the wheels turn.

On a dirt track entering a turn, the drivers pull the steering wheel to the right then quickly back to the left, to get the car sideways so they can slide through the curve. Deliberately throwing themselves in a skid. Then coming out of the turn they hit the gas for the straight away.

Renee is up in the third heat race. Her qualifying time put her in the second row. Lon Chambers picks her up and drops her between the cage of roll bars welded to the car.

Someone puts a beer in my hand. I don't take my eyes off the track. Racing is exciting when you know a driver. I don't want to miss a moment.

The cars zip past us leaving a trail of dust. Her blue C9 is a blur. In the middle of turn three on the fifth lap, her right rear tire hits a rut.

All four wheels come off the track.

The car flies twenty feet in the air.

Turns over and over.

People scream.

I'm too scared to breathe.

She flips the guard rail.

We jump to our feet to get a better view.

The car lands on its side in a corn field outside the track.

Is she hurt?

I'm biting my lip when I'm pulled up so I can stand on the bench.

Cars stop around the track.

Jim sprints out on to the track. He is followed by the emergency guys.

When they reach the top of the high bank Renee is sitting on the guard rail taking off her helmet.

He picks her up and starts shaking her. Yelling at her.

She slaps him.

"The driver is okay folks. Popped him one."

There is sigh of relief in Matt's voice over the loud speaker.

"Come on, Abel. Lets go get the war wagon, so we can help Lon get the car back in shape for her to drive in the feature."

Chapter 19

It was prime racing. Locals hadn't seen anything like it. They're still exclaiming in amazement at how fast midget sprint cars can go around the track as we follow them to the parking lot. They're accustomed to watching cumbersome muscle cars, lumber across the finish line.

"Evan, Abel Young had a gun under his jacket."

"He's a sheriff. Law requires him to wear a gun."

"When he is off duty?"

"Out of his jurisdiction. He's never off duty."

"You're a private investigator. You don't carry a gun."

"Petra, in the eyes of the law, I'm like you, a private citizen. If I wore a gun on my hip in plain view, like in western movies, it would look stupid, but it's not illegal. Concealed weapons are a different stripe."

"He was carrying an expensive camera."

"Abel? Never seen him without one. It was a Yashica, works better in low light. He has forgotten more about taking pictures than I'll ever know. He was the medic attached to our patrol in Vietnam. Didn't carry a gun then, just his camera and medical bag."

"In a war? Is he a conscientious objector?"

"Not so I noticed. Didn't say he couldn't use a weapon. One time he was working on a guy. The Cong kept taking pot shots at him so he couldn't do his job. Got irritated from having to duck so often and lost his temper. Grabbed the guy's rifle to lay down a line of well placed shots. When Abel Young's riled he can drive ten penny nails at 300 yards and not waste a bullet."

"Did you see it?"

"It was my rifle."

The rest of the way home, Petra peppers me with dozens of questions I'm hard put to answer. The brat's sharp and absorbs information like a sponge. She'd watched every race, but was disappointed when Renee didn't win.

Explain to her a fifth in a 200 lap race from last place the first time out against experienced male drivers 's a respectable finish for a girl. She puffs up at my remark as if she considers gender and experience of no importance in winning races.

She and Renee hit it off right at the start. Ate their way through four loaded chili dogs. Then shared an elephant ear, getting powder sugar smeared to their ears.

It's pushing on midnight as I pull into the garage beside my place. Whoof's barking and whining to be let out. Been pinned up for over eight hours.

"Coming. Coming, boy. Hold it one more minute."

Open the door to his desperate signals. He doesn't greet me. Bolts out the door, racing toward the river.

Flip the light switch. Not only does my place smell of flea dip, it's a shambles. My frantic dog had used the bed as a trampoline, trying to get out the high windows. At 120 pounds he's made a royal mess.

Bend over to pick up scattered papers. Wet dog lands on my back knocking me flat. Roll over to throw off the dripping mongrel. He isn't having it. Clamps his teeth on my jacket and pulls me up, then takes off out the door.

Smell of flea dipped soaking dog. Damn. He's been in the river.

Hates the river!

Lake is fine. Nothing this side of hell will force him in the river.

Reach for my flashlight and race after him. There's something in the river he needs me to see.

Cast the beam across the muddy water. Flick it back and forth till I catch him in its light. Shallow near the bank. Whoof churned up silt before taking the plunge. Rotten fish pervades the night air.

My dog's having a hard time fighting the current and pulling a bundle of old clothes. Holding the flashlight high, I wade in to help him rescue his booty.

The moment I touch his catch. I know…a body.

Sam's.

There's no mistaking the old green plaid shirt even if it's wet.

Between us we get him out on the bank. Turn him over to try CPR. His brown eyes are wide open, staring at the sky.

He's been shot.

There's a bullet hole between the buttons.

"Stay. Guard."

Stumble up what's left of the old loading dock after last winter's flood and call Maddy. Then the police.

Grab my Yashica. While I'm waiting for them to arrive, I take a roll of shots. Check the flop house. Spick and span like always. Yippi and the kid are no where to be seen.

Coming out the door when Billy Ray Johnson pulls in. His lights flashing. City ambulance behind him with sirens blaring. I point them around back and follow.

Point to Sam's body. Inform them Whoof and I pulled him out of the river.

It's dark down there. They'll have to bring in big lights on stands to work.

Billy Ray follows me back to my place. I can give them a little help by throwing on security lights mounted on the sides of the warehouse.

"He catch a break in?"

"No. This mess 's an attempt to break out. Whoof was penned up in here while I was in Richmond at the races. He knew something was going down. Tried to get out."

"May we use some of your outlets for the extension cords to our lights?"

"Sure, just don't overload and trip the breakers."

"Going to be a long night."

"I'll go make a pot of coffee. Sam'll have donuts in the freezer."

"Thanks, we'll need it."

When I get the coffee going and step outside, Maddy has arrived. She and Billy Ray are going at it.

"Mrs. Sorals, a murder scene is no place for you."

"Sam?"

"Ma'am, We can't be sure until we notify the next of kin and get a positive identification."

"Samuel Lester Sorals. I'm next of kin. My brother. I'm going down?"

"No ma'am. I can't allow you down there. It's a crime scene."

Billy Ray's missing signals.

Maddy's stark still. Face cold. Dark eyes – blank. Ready to scatter Billy Ray, in little pieces, across the parking lot.

Put my hand on her shoulder. The tension she holds back scorches.

"Maddy, they've a job to do. Let them have at it.

"We can watch from the steps. You can see him when they bring up his body.

"Whoof found him."

I look around. Where's Whoof? He's not underfoot. A soft whimper comes from the shadows of the warehouse.

His coat blends with the dark to be near invisible. I catch the glow of his eyes. He's parked against the ironwork that covers the door to the crawl space.

Wretched night wears on. Maddy frozen in shock. Put a cup of coffee in her hand, which she ignores.

When the guys wheel the gurney up the bank, she walks over and lifts the sheet. Then nods to Billy Ray.

Silence's eerie. No one talking, no bird calls, no fish flopping in the river, nor crunch of feet walking on fresh gravel.

We stand by the drive like a sentinel honor guard as Billy Ray, followed by the ambulance, pull away.

A grey mist of fog settles around us.

"I'll drive you home."

"No. Evan, what you can do is make sure no one goes digging in Sam's past.

"Take care of the place.

"Sam was my last link to any family I ever had. He was a good man. I will find out who killed him and take care of it."

Believe every word she says. Retribution for murder's a mountain code, which has no equal.

Gross amateur could read the sign of what happened. Someone was trying to get into my place. Sam caught him and tried to stop it. He was shot at point blank range. The river didn't wash away the fine burn holes in his shirt.

Killer dragged his body down the slope and dumped it in the river. What he didn't count on was it bumping up against the old loading ramp under the water instead of drifting on down stream.

Isn't a good time to tell her she has a spy in her cleaning service

~ ~ ~

Clean up the leftover coffee and sugar crumbs in the shelter. Leave it like Sam would have expected.

Still no Whoof. He's a donut hound. Can smell them a mile away. Need to rescue what he has cornered in the crawl space.

"What have you caught? Move."

Open the door and shine my flashlight into the opening. As I surmised – one mud covered dog and the kid.

"Come on out. Everyone's gone."

Miserable looking pair emerge. Both are covered with mud.

Ground under the warehouse's still wet from the flood. Sam kept the openings wide during the day to let them air out. It's a slow process. Flooding hadn't been as bad up river where we are, but enough to get under the building. This last time, Capital City had gotten it twice, within a period of ten days.

Learned why the windows of the warehouse are high and the walls triple brick thick. It was built to withstand the river during floods. Before trucks, a distiller depended on the river for everything.

Kid has Yippi in a death grip. No wonder he hadn't barked during the long night.

"Come on, there's some coffee and donuts in the refrigerator.

You can tell me why you hid."

"Figured they'd think I did it."

"Don't be an idiot. Not holding Sam's dog. Yippi and Whoof would have mauled, not protected you."

Unlock the shelter and shoved them through the door. Whoof prancing beside them. His sensitive nose has detected the scent of sweets.

"While I reheat the coffee, get a shower. Take Yippi with you. He needs one too. Clean clothes in the storage room. Don't leave a mess."

"Know where they are. Don't need your orders."

He's sullen and scared. I ignore him.

I'm sitting at the table smoking one of Sam's little cigars when they emerge from the shower room. Kid's face's still swollen. Black and blue marks fading to greenish-yellow pasted across his pale skin. His eyes, now that I can see them, are a bright blue. Absent the dirt, his hair's a pale sun bleached blonde.

There's bruising down his pencil thin arms. His knuckles skinned. He'd fought back. No wonder he'd run from who ever worked him over.

Reaches for the packet of cigars. Stop him.

"Too young. What's your name?"

"Rusty Russell."

"Rusty, you clean up real good. Now eat before Whoof forgets his manners and demolishes those sweet rolls."

He walks over to the cabinet above the sink and takes down a small plate, gathers up a napkin and a fork from the counter.

Takes two rolls on the plate. Carefully cuts one into one-third, two third portions. The dogs sit at attention beside his chair. He gives them their share. They lay down and don't beg for more.

Be a piss poor detective if I couldn't see they'd shared this ritual before. Ah, Sam gave Whoof a treat before he put him up, after his early evening run.

Rusty cuts his roll and takes small bites. Could be loose teeth from the beating he endured. Though it looks as if somewhere the kid has been taught how to eat in company. Join him instead of picking one up and taking a bite. Don't want to embarrass him or let him know I see any thing unusual in his behavior.

He cleans the table, pours us a second cup of coffee, and reaches for the packet.

He's testing me. Don't stop him.

First draw betrays him. You don't smoke a cigar like a cigarette. Sam's cigars have the flavor of tar paper rolled in raw tobacco. It's a valiant try. He soon puts it out, in the ash tray beside mine. Not much for smoking either, though I do carry a pack of Camels or Viceroys for clients during an interview.

Learn a few things my earlier summary missed. Rusty and the dogs were down by the river, chasing sticks when Sam called Whoof, to put him in my place, which he did.

They were coming up the bank when a man came around the corner from the parking lot. Sam was heading back to the shelter, when the guy struck him from behind with a club. Yippi and Whoof started barking. Rusty grabbed Yippi to keep him quiet and hid on the far side against the building.

Peeking over the steps, Rusty saw the man turn Sam over and shoot him. Yippi and Whoof were raising hell. The man tugged Sam down the slope and dumped him in the river.

When his back was turned, Rusty got the iron gate to the crawl space open, crawled in, and watched. The man took off up river in a johnboat he had hidden in the willows.

Sam was his friend. He hadn't meant to hide from the police. Whoof parked against the gate. He couldn't open the door. He swore the dogs kept talking to each other.

167

Imagination? Suppose it's possible they've known each other for four years. In fact, it was Yippi who hauled a half drowned pup the same size as he, out of the river.

"We'll sleep over here. Whoof trashed my place trying to get out."

~ ~ ~

Whoof had learned his lesson about cots and settles down on the floor. Yippi isn't getting a yard from Rusty so they're fast asleep in minutes.

Sleep's the last thing on my mind.

Have Maddy getting set for a vendetta. She will run rough shod over the City Police, call in every marker she can dig up, and turn this town upside down until she finds Sam's killer. Then, blood on the moon won't be a figure of speech when she's finished.

What did she mean by her remark of making sure no one looked in Sam's past?

Sam Sorals was a good man who'd spent the last twenty or so years giving a leg-up to anyone who was short in the stirrup. He'd worked untold hours, rescuing people during the last flood. Feeding them, housing them, and pitching in to clean up the broken lives the waters left behind. He had no bones about drafting all the recruits he could lay his hands on, to help with his projects.

Want to find the bastard who killed him. Doubt Maddy will arrive soon enough to deliver the benediction. It hurts too much when I look at the bunk next to me.

My clean clothes are all laid out ready for delivery.

Have my promise to Clayton to honor, to keep Petra safe and I'd taken his money. No one can give her back the parents she doesn't remember.

Have TT barking at my heels, to find his sister's murderer and to stop blocking his access to his niece.

Three of the deaths have a connection somewhere in a twisted mind. Sam and Clayton's shootings indicate they had the rotten luck to have stumbled into a bad scene at the wrong time. Doesn't make Sam any less dead or Clayton less down.

Now have a kid who's been worked over rough rails and a dog with a lost master. Kid who'd seen Sam killed, but didn't see the man's face.

In anybody's book, Rusty's a material witness and legally should be turned over to Billy Ray. Once it becomes known there's a witness to Sam's death the killer will return.

Have an idea. Isn't legal, in fact if I look hard enough I'll find I'm committing a crime, if not several.

No one knows Rusty exists. He's going to the lake to get the chance to fish, ride a bicycle, and watch girls in bathing suits like any normal boy his age. Whatever it may be.

Wedge's keeping tabs on Petra when we arrive at

McIntyre's the next morning. The twins have set up a watch station on the balcony porch, which gives them a view of the river, back area of the house and side street where the house fronts. One of them slips out the wall gate of the garden for a foot patrol of the front at irregular intervals.

He tells me she has taken to sleeping in a back bedroom near where they have their station.

Open the French doors and send Whoof back to guard duty. He doesn't mind. Brat has a wide bed and Charity keeps treats in the pantry.

Delegate Wedge to take Rusty to the lake and deposit him on my houseboat.

Kid starts to protest about my underhanded tricks. Takes one look at Wedge when he hauls freight out of the rocking chair and changes his mind.

Rusty isn't the first to decide Wedge's one person you don't want to mess with, under any circumstance. I sweeten the trip by giving Wedge money to feed him and take him shopping for clothes and necessities on the trip down.

Intruder on her territory isn't going to sit well with my foster daughter, Bobbi Vance. But she'll have to learn to live with it. When I'm not around she lives in the farmhouse above the marina with Anvil and Doris Forge.

Anvil's the proud father of a boy. Welding Forge should keep her busy and off the docks until I get a chance to get down there to settle their living arrangements.

Not a good solution. It's the best I can do until the police or I find a killer.

How in the hell did I get saddled with three stubborn kids and an extra dog?

Have a drudgery day cut out for me. Pi's idea of PI work's one colored by Sam Spade or one of the other cop shows on TV, where all the pieces fall into place in an hour or so. Real life doesn't come anywhere near what those programs crack it up to be.

Need to get one of the tourist maps from the city building of the historical section of the city to give me an idea of the layout of the area. So far what I know is what I've learned from driving around, looking for a place to hide my truck.

Do some digging at the public library. Look through old city cross directories to see who lived in the area when Clara Dialman and McIntyre were murdered.

Fifteen years 's a long time. If I'm armed with some names who are still around I can knock on a few doors. Papers TT gave me didn't include any reports of interviews with Dialman's neighbors. Someone might remember something the police didn't discover.

Chapter 20

Haven't had a full night's sleep in three days. Down past the refuel mark and running on empty.

Park my truck four streets back from the river, in an old stable the Beautification League's petitioning the city council to demolish to create a small park. Their petition's under fire from the Historical Society because the stable once belonged to a founding father.

Ames said it's part of the Dialman estate. I'll leave the preservationists in his hands. It's perfect for keeping my truck out of sight.

Nothing can be done until the estate's settled. Hence my hidy-hole stands, though a good wind will solve all their problems.

One place to hide's Clayton's pad above the garage. Intend to use it for the next 24 hours with the phone unplugged. Whoof could find me, but he won't leave his post guarding Petra unless given his release command.

Have an old satchel packed with fresh clothes and shaving gear. Don't use another man's razor.

Cut down by the river and take the alley running behind her house turning over the events of a long day in my mind. I'll have to write it out in long hand. My typewriter's at the warehouse.

Head explodes.

World goes black.

~ ~ ~

Flat on my face. Spitting gavel.

Fumes of motor oil mixed with blood.

Rough tongue of small dog rasps my neck.

Head hurts as if I'm coming off a ten day drunk.

Lift it to see where I am.

Gravel spins in a whirling spiral.

From a long way off a kid's voice keeps breaking into a high pitch scream in my ear.

"Wake up!

"Don't die!

"Please wake up."

Sharp static of dog barks.

"No, Yippie. No."

Wave my hand in a limp fashion. Get my arms under me to rise.

Thin arms go around me so tight I can barely breathe.

Manage to get to my hands and knees, rocking back and forth like a hobby horse.

Eyes go in and out of focus. Fog off the river.

Someone grilled a steak near by.

Get enough momentum going to flop up on my butt.

Cold cocked.

Rolled like a greenhorn.

Contents of my billfold are scattered. Reach for it and almost totter over before I'm pushed up right.

Kid picks up the cards. Stuffing them back in my wallet. Hands it to me.

"Didn't take your money. Yippie tried to bite him. He kicked him. Grabbed your bag and ran."

"Which way?"

"River."

Over the pounding in my skull I hear the faint whine of an outboard motor pushed to it's limits heading out.

Warm stream running down my face. Put a shaky hand up and touch near my ear.

God, wish I hadn't.

Stabbing pains chase each other across my eyes.

"Handkerchief in back pocket…can't reach. Get it."

Dog jumps in my lap. Licking my face. Make a move to push him away. Touch a pelt the texture of a scrub brush.

Yippi, Sam's dog.

The kid, Rusty. What the hell? Sent him to the lake with Wedge.

Hurt more than I care to admit.

Anger floods me.

"How did you get here?"

"Back of your truck. Followed from the shack."

"How…?"

"Crawled over from Sam's side on the rafters."

"Yippi?"

"Zipped him in my jacket."

"Damn fool. Asking for a punched ticket. Why did you come back?"

"Ain't taking orders from no shrimp."

Afraid of Bobbi. Kid knows a witch lurks in women, even nine year-olds.

"Figures. Give me a hand."

Struggle. Make it to a wobbly stance.

Put my arm across his shoulders. Feel his bones through my jacket.

Earth takes a new spine.

With his help I manage to stay erect.

"Did you see it?"

"Yeah."

"And?"

"Man who killed Sam hit you with a baseball bat. It's over there. Want me to get it? "

"No, leave it. Evidence. Police 'll pick it up."

"Cops, no way."

"Right. You nor Yippi will be within miles."

We stagger up the alley to the gate. Let go and collapse.

"Quiet. Careful. Climb over.

"Unlatch the gate. Don't wake the neighbors."

He scrambles up the wall like it's a boardwalk. Disappears. Moments later the gate opens. He holds it with his foot. Helps me to my feet.

We go up the stairs backwards, with me on my ass. Have to make a couple of stops. Arms give out.

Take my keys. Find the right one with a couple of misses and push him through the door.

No help for it. Flip on a light. Shades still down.

"Over there." Point to the chair.

Balance against the edge of the cot. He fools with the lever on the recliner. Surprised when the footrest shoots out and the back goes down. Yippi jumps on his lap and curls in a ball.

"Got to clean up. Stay there. Don't move. No noise."

Strip. Toss ruined clothes in a pile by the door. Dig through Clayton's stuff for a change.

Still dizzy. Better. Check in the mirror. Head wounds bleed like the dickens. Aren't serious. Winch every time I feel for a cracked skull.

Concussion, maybe. Smashed ear. Skin around my left eye starting to blacken.

Climb in the shower, lean against the wall, and take the water as hot as I can stand. Dry off, struggle to fasten a pair of jeans. Manage to pull a t-shirt over my ear without screaming.

Clayton has some square bandages and tape. Rub the steam off the mirror. Bleeding's stopped. Apply rough first-aid over the worst of the damage.

Rusty and Yippi out cold. Under new layers of grim the bruising on his face's fading. Both need a bath. Don't have the heart to disturb 'em. They pulled me out of a tight spot.

Beer bottle's beside the chair. Damn brat took the last one. Pick it up – more than half full. Finish it.

His battered boots lie on their sides. One has papers sticking out of it. Being a master at prying I don't hesitate. Read them and get a shock. Birth certificate and a marriage license.

Lunge for the phone so fast I come near falling. Dial Curt Colton's unlisted number.

He's as groggy as I am when he picks up.

"Yeah."

"Get over to your office on the double."

"Are you drunk?"

"Don't know. No arguments. Got a problem. It's time you start meddling."

"See you as soon as I can get there."

Shake Rusty.

"Come on. Move it. We're out of here."

~ ~ ~

177

I obey every traffic regulation to the letter heading across town. It's a dead give away of a drunk driving. Can't afford to be stopped in my condition.

Rusty isn't saying a word. Glance at him. Gone back to sleep. Kid has all the signs of exhaustion. Know them well.

When I pull in front of the barracks, he sits up.

"You said no fuzz. This is the top cop shop."

"Not letting you out of my sight. Need to see a man about getting banged.

"Get out. Bring Yippi so he won't raise a racket while we're gone. Help me to the door. Keep your mouth shut."

Steer him down the hall with my hand on his shoulder. Needs some meals. No kid should be this skinny. Nothing but skin covered bones.

Curt's sitting behind his desk fiddling with a paper knife. Half dressed and blazing.

Push Rusty down in a chair and prop myself on the edge of his desk so my butt hides his name plate.

"What in the hell?"

"Calm down. I'll explain."

"You haul me out of bed at four in the morning. March in here hauling a dirty kid, sporting a smashed ear. Looking like a punch drunk fighter on his last legs, then have the nerve to tell me to calm down. Friendship has its limits."

"You made a point. In no condition to drive. Call one of your cars. Have them pick me up out front to take me back to the warehouse when I'm finished."

"Like hell you will. I'm calling Maddy to have you checked in Stoddard's. Getting to be a revolving bed out there for knights without armor."

Dialing the phone before I can stop him. Not a bad idea…he's getting fuzzy.

"Surrender. Listen to me."

Don't give him a chance to work up another head of steam.

"Rusty's a material witness. His old man sold him into an 'apprenticeship' in Fog Landing. Master worked him over. How he made it to Sam's, I don't know. You get it out of him."

"Not talking to no fuzz."

"Told you to keep your mouth shut. Get back in that chair. Stay there."

Patience with numbskulls is kaput.

"I've got one nitwit brat on my hands to keep alive. Can't keep track of two. Get it through that thick skull of yours this guy's playing for keeps."

Back to Curt I come near falling off the desk. Bad business, the beer's making me lightheaded.

"Bright boy here watched a guy put a bullet in Sam Sorals. Then, saw me get slammed with a bat. It's in the alley near McIntyre's gate. Have one of yours pick it up before someone else finds it.

"Morning after Sam was killed, I sent him with Wedge to the lake to keep him safe. Had a turf dispute with Bobbi and high-tailed it back, in time to see same guy get me.

"Admit I'd be dead if Yippi…Sam's dog hadn't tried to take a bite out of the bastard.

"Rolled me. Took satchel and notebook. Didn't get anything, but clothes. Fresh book.

"Put this kid in a holding cell. Handcuff him to the bed frame. Feed him.

"Idiot climbs like a squirrel. Doesn't know how to tell the truth. Slippery as a greased pig."

"Am not. Leveled with you."

"Rusty, keep quiet before I add a few bruises to your collection. Everyone in town knows Yippi belonged to old Sam."

"Evan, I told you I can't enter a city case without probable cause."

"It's time you meddle. You've got a railcar full of 'probable causes.'

"Lieutenant Curtis Burton Colton"

Climb off the desk. Start for the door.

"Meet Neal Colton Russell. Your nephew. Proof in his boot."

Walk out and slam the door.

Chapter 21

Same doctor who worked on Clayton's waiting at Stoddard's when Curt's guys dump me at the door.

Doc doesn't give me anything stronger than aspirin. Hooks up a glucose IV. Tells me to stay awake as much as possible.

Stands there a moment observing the stitches he'd taken in my scalp. Was able to answer him when he asked if I minded enduring a bit of patch work, without a pain killer.

Ear, he pieces together with metal clips much like alligator clips. Tells me they will leave less scaring. Grin up at him like a fool thinking about areas of my hide under the sheet resembling a battle zone. Abel Young had patched me up more than once and declared me fit for duty.

Doc takes a longer survey of me and changes his mind. Says some sleep shouldn't hurt. Ring the bell if the dizziness returns.

Grateful the double vision has cleared up. Had me worried. My job would be hell if I'd see two of everything.

Maddie arrives. Whoof's beside her. Tells the Doc she'll stay with me. Checks me over with the efficiency of an Army nurse.

Stuffs a banana in my mouth. Takes the skin and spreads it around my eye.

"What are you doing?"

"Shut up. Best medicine I know for bruising. I've spent plenty of time treating them."

She promises if I don't live she'll kill me. Demands I tell her everything.

Try. I drift in and out, like Clayton.

Hear her crying. Maddy doesn't cry. She's one tough lady.

"Sam drowned. He was alive when the son-of-a-bitch dumped him in the river. Billy Ray called me. Bullet is the same as killed Dialman and the one Doc dug out of Clayton."

Brain's beginning to work.

"Brat?"

Try to get up. She pushes me back in the bed.

"Desper and Charity are in the house. She is safe."

"Wedge?"

"Sleeping."

"Maddy, check your people. TT's getting information that had to have come from your sources."

"I'll take care of it."

"Anyone volunteers to help with Pi…nail 'em."

"Don't worry. We'll handle it. Billy Ray is real helpful."

Wondered what she has on him or traded for information. Let it pass.

"What did you mean about Sam's past?"

"I was upset."

Overhead light glows green. Bile rises in my throat.

"Maddy, john. Going to throw up."

"Don't give me that."

"Honest. Help me up."

"Hold it. Puke is one mess I'm not cleaning up."

Pitch every cookie I hadn't eaten. Drift back to sleep. When I wake up she starts where we left off.

"It isn't important now. Twenty years ago, Sam got arrested for a robbery he didn't commit. Sheriff in the mountains intended to hang a long prison term on him, to get himself reelected. Took one of my girls up there. She gave the sheriff a blow job, while I swiped his keys and got Sam out of there. Locked the old bastard in Sam's cell.

"He hid at my place till the heat died. I bought the old warehouse. Sam fixed it up for other guys – in trouble and has been living low ever since.

"When I had my house, he made sure no one caused a ruckus to bring the police.

"When you live on the fringes, you need someone to watch your back. Sam watched mine."

Taking Whoof with her, she bars the door for 24 hours. Takes my clothes to make sure I stay. Not my clothes I'd been wearing, Clayton's.

Sleep broken by a brief visit for a breakfast from Turleys delivered by Curt with a clean Rusty and Yippi in tow. The kid doesn't say much, but stares wide-eyed at the bruising and where the doctor shaved the side of my head to repair my ear.

"Here is your hat. Found it under a bush near the ball bat. Same bat used on Sam Sorals. Blood stains in the wood gave the lab boy good samples. No prints."

He hangs it on a hook beside the door. I'd been in too much pain to miss my battered leather planter's hat.

"Extensive fact finding. Man's a coward."

"How do you figure?"

"Can't do much except think while I'm parked. Strikes from behind in the dark."

"Now that you mention it, murder is the way cowards solve problems."

"Sam and I were hit with the same bat."

"True."

"He's shorter than I am. Look, the end of the bat hit my ear. Got Sam straight out across the back of the head. Took photos of his body before Johnson arrived."

"Does Johnson know?"

"It's none of his business. They were for my files. His guy did the same, I watched him."

"Get some rest, the shiner is a beauty. Goes with your face."

As they leave Curt pats my shoulder.

"Thanks. We'll talk when Maddy gives you parole.

"I owe you a big one. Will see what I can unofficially dig up without stepping on Johnson's toes."

Whoof proceeds dinner with a flying leap to the bed and stands over me, licking my face. Send him to the foot. His breath smells like one of Pat's burgers complete with onions.

Desper's holding one of Bihn's boxes and laughing.

"Knew you were here the minute we pulled in the parking lot."

Pi comes over to the bed and studies my face.

"Did he try to kill you?"

"Don't know. My hat deflected the blow."

"Lieutenant Colton alerted us. We went over to stay with Miss Petra till you get back on the job."

"Maddy promised to bring me some clothes in the morning. I'm okay. Swelling and bruising will fade. Glancing blow put me out for a spell.

"Lucky the guy's shorter than I am. It would never have happened if I'd been paying attention when I came up the alley."

"Charity cleaned the apartment and disposed of your dirty clothes. I helped her."

185

"Desper, check my place. Maddy has the keys. Haven't had time to clean up there, either.

"Get your nose out of my supper, you worthless hound. You had yours. Smell you."

"Mr. Bihn is very nice. He didn't charge us for Whoof's supper. He ate two burgers and most of my home fries."

I'll tell Pat he's been described as a 'nice guy.' He'll enjoy it. She'll never have to pay for a burger the rest of her life.

~ ~ ~

I finished writing my letter to Mrs. Strove. She loves to get letters. Strovie's favorites are about birds and flowers. I don't mention the ugly things which have happened. Mickie Stiles, her next door neighbor will read it to her and write her reply.

I sent her a postcard with a picture of the Capitol Building on it after I arrived. She had Mickie send me one of Chesapeake Bay. Her card is the only mail I've gotten besides bills.

Whoof is stretched across my bed with his head resting on Dumbo. He looks so sad. Every time a car passes on the street his ears perk up as if he is listening for Mr. Blade's truck.

I don't want doggie hair all over Dumbo. I reach for him and Whoof clamps his teeth around his trunk.

"No, no Whoof. I'm not playing. Dumbo isn't your toy."

The harder I pull the harder he pulls back. This stupid dog thinks I'm playing tug-a-war with him.

I bat his nose to make him let go. He throws his head up pulling me off the floor. I hear a rip and fall.

Poor dog. Dumbo's nose came off. He shakes his head and looks at me. I slap him hard. His stupid game ruined my friend.

Whoof jumps down from the bed and cringes, on the floor beside my foot like he's afraid of me.

I'm shaking as I pick up the battered nose. Matron insisted I learn to sew. Charity will know where I can find a needle and thread in the house. Every house has a sewing basket somewhere for little repairs.

My old friend looks so forlorn, tattered and torn. Shorn of his nose by a bad dog. Old different colored threads dangle from the nose. Dumbo lost his nose before.

Blue stuffing is bulging out of his body. Velvet – a blue velvet bag. I empty the bag on the bed. Jewelry…glittering, pretty jewelry falls on the coverlet.

I run my fingers through the trove like I'm Captain Kidd who has opened a long lost treasure chest. A rope of pearls all the same size, a gold bracelet with deep purple amethysts (my birthstone) surrounded by diamonds, an Indian designed silver bracelet with a center stone like veined marble, and a watch on a heavy gold chain with a cameo on the front side, tumble though my fingers.

There are three pairs of earrings, greenish grey pearls the size of marbles, diamond solitaire studs that look to be about a karat, and plain gold hoops. Five rings fit my middle finger. One, a gold band engraved with flowers, leaves, and vines. The gold has a rose-colored tint and the design is worn, someone's treasured wedding ring. It feels old.

A heavy silver ring, badly tarnished mounting like an open lotus blossom, the single stone gleams a reddish purple. When I take it to the window for a better look, it turns a deep blue green. I've never seen another like it.

A pearl ring matches the earrings. Their mounting aren't tarnished like silver. It's white gold. The solitaire diamond is large, though not vulgar and obviously an engagement ring.

A dark brown oval topaz, set sideways with a spray of small diamonds curving around one side and a high school class ring that fits my thumb.

The final piece is a diamond necklace of fine filagree. The round stones are scattered at random. In the center of the 'v' is a pear shaped diamond, like a large tear drop. A piece designed for an elegant ballroom.

I stand by the bed, looking at the treasures. They belonged to my mother. I know they did. Hidden in Dumbo's body she left them for me to find when she gave me away.

The tall chest between the lights was made to hold treasures. I pull the desk chair over and climb up to place the pieces on the dark velvet. My silver cross pin from high school and the Navy insignia tie tack I'd picked up on the parade ground, don't look lost anymore amid the splendor.

One day I'll have a chance to wear her lovely things. I'll wear them with pride. She loved me.

Chapter 22

Ames looks me over with a critical eye. The bruising has faded to a yellowish stain, hair where it was shaved's GI, the ear requires a small patch. My hat's cocked to the right.

"No idea who laid you out?"

"No, I do know it's the same guy who murdered Sam Sorals. There's indication he killed McIntyre, Dialman and a Mrs. Emmens plus put a bullet in Clayton."

"Are you sure?"

"The police don't have a gun, but the bullets are the same."

"Why attack you?"

"Two options. One I'm blocking his way to Petra or two he thinks I have something he wants. My guess he was attempting to break in my place when Sam stumbled on him. He trashed both Dialman and McIntyre's places looking for something."

Ames opens his briefcase. Hands me a folder.

"Mary found this in her aunt's papers. Read it."

Folder contains a single sheet of expensive stationary bearing Marcus McIntyre's letterhead.

Letter signed by him details rumors circulating of a pedophile operating in Capital City. He did not know the identity of the person nor who gave him the information. He promises to continue searching. He'd included two newspaper articles reporting the bodies of children pulled from the river near Fog Landing. One clipping was eighteen years-old. The second dated twenty years back.

Reporter theorized they were foundlings as no children had been reported missing in the area. The president of the board of directors of the Valley View Children's Home, T. T. Towbridge assured him, after having Mrs. Florence Emmens, the matron view both bodies, the children had never been residents of their facility.

Connections adding like numbers on a calculator. Rusty – Fog Landing – Sam – Pi – Valley View Children's Home – Mrs. Emmens murdered. TT in the middle. Curt was wrong.

"Good morning, gentleman."

His voice at my elbow knocks me into next week. Without thinking I blurt.

"Where's Rusty?"

"At the lake."

"He ran."

"Idea good. Lousy strategy. He'll stay this time. Has a job."

"Too young. Has to be fourteen to get a work permit. What job?"

"Harbor Master for the summer. He'll be fourteen in August."

"Run that by me again."

"You heard me. Safe out of town. Wedge worked out a deal with Miss McIntyre for the marina. Found a house trailer on pontoons. Using it to make a snack bar and grocery to link the docks. Rusty is staying on it while helping the twins with the conversion. Pumps gas, directs docking, and keeps the boats in order. Too busy to fight with Bobbi."

"Who is Rusty?"

"My nephew. Evan found him. His parents are dead. Father died and his mother, my sister, remarried a guy by the name of Foreman Otis from Fog Landing. Turned out he was a wife-beating wine-o. Family lost track of her. She died of cancer. Otis was stuck with a kid not his own. Sold him for booze."

"I see."

"No, Ames, you don't. Could lose my job. Rusty watched Sam Sorals' murder and saw Blade get slammed by the same guy. Didn't see his face, just the action. Legally, he is a material witness and I haven't reported it.

"I didn't know he existed until Evan hauled him into my office. I'll be damned if I'll let my own nephew be killed by a maniac, covering his tracks or any other kid for that matter."

"Which brings us to Petra McIntyre, another throw away kid."

"The brat is no kid."

"No, but she was when Clayton stashed her in the children's home. She was a victim in one sense and a potential victim in another, who is innocent of any crime. Besides being helpless."

"Worst mistake Clayton ever made."

"What do you mean?"

"She's as helpless as a boa constrictor. Those homes are an early training ground for con artists. To survive, the kids become chamaeleons, changing personalities to fit what they perceive's expected of them. Knew a passel of 'em on the carney circuit my folks worked.

"Old man Thornton lied to authorities to keep me out of one. Claimed I was his grandson when he didn't know if I even had a name. Never called me anything except 'boy.'"

"Of course, he knew your name. He was your great-uncle."

Round on Curt, ready to bust his chops.

"What are you talking about?"

"Your name, Evan Aloysius Blade. When you were in California hiding out, my uncle thought it was time for your charade to end. Gave me your birth certificate. It was in Mr. Thornton's Bible.

"Uncle Ben bought it at the sale. Elroy Harris told me to send it to a Monsignor Brian Stanley to straighten out your mess as he had friends in high places.

"Mr. Thornton's sister, Alberta married a half-breed Cherokee, David Blade. Her parents disowned her. Their son, Paul Thornton Blade was your father."

Stunned. Can't say a word. Why in the hell had no one bothered to tell me?

Curt's shaking my shoulder.

"I'm sorry. I assumed you knew."

"Why…why did he lie?"

"To protect you. Didn't want to rake up an old scandal. When did he give you the moniker?"

"Day I started school."

"Makes sense. Kids are cruel. They repeat what they hear their parents say. You left…your parents never said anything?"

"No. Moved around. Week was a long run. Were wintering in Parkersburg, West Virginia, when my draft notice found me. Never saw them again."

Place's empty. Feels like it's crowded. Got accustomed to people staring at me because of my nose. Their eyes moving fast as if they're embarrassed to be caught seeing me. This 's different. It's like someone's walking on my soul.

"Thanks, Curt. Talk when we visit Rusty. Know where there's an old Chris Craft runabout, I've had my eye on. He can fix it up in his spare time."

They understand. Close the subject.

"Johnson is hunting two guys who broke into the courthouse. Do you know anything about it?"

Ames' lopsided grin peeks around a slice of toast.

"Bihn told us while we were having Manhattans. I had to foot the bill. Said Whoof had maxed out his tab."

"If you say so."

"I do. He never spent thirty years of long nights at sea. My crew would have cleaned him out in an hour. I'm rusty. Took longer.

"I have an appointment. Shall we get back to matters at hand. Give Curt the letter.

"Mary's aunt, Ophelia Laurence and Marcus McIntyre were first cousins. Her father and his mother were brother and sister. They operated a type of underground railroad to hide abused women and children. The letter and clippings were in a collection of correspondence from him."

Hand the folder to Curt. Take a drink of cold coffee. Tastes like curdled milk left out for a week. While he's reading I signal the waitress to bring us a fresh pot. Point to my cold stack. She takes the hint and brings me a fresh serving with hot syrup.

As he reads, Curt drums his fingers on the table in a syncopated rhythm missing a few beats here and there.

"How far is Fog Landing up river from Creelsboro?"

"Fifty or sixty miles at least, if not more. Why?"

"Remember Peter Faulks?"

195

"Who'd forget. Thought about him when I went back to see Mr. Thornton's grave."

"I don't mean the hanging. Peter as a person. How he looked?"

"Curt, what were we? Six…seven years old?"

"In between? Think back. Peter was blonde, curly hair. Pretty for a boy. Molested."

"My God, you're saying this guy has been raping kids for over twenty-five years?"

"Wondering. Ties in. My dad never stopped hunting for Peter's killer after Odie Simpson was lynched for a crime he didn't commit. He hated the ugly blot on his hometown. People moved. Your parents took you. My parents sent me to KMI."

"KMI?"

"Kentucky Military Institute. The majority of guys were there because they were bad actors. Boys their parents couldn't control who had enough money to keep them out of reform school. A training ground for thugs. To survive you had to learn to fight back and fight dirty.

"One school few put on a resume if they want a legitimate job. It got me my Army lieutenant's rank."

Never mentioned where he went to school. Figured he'd had the privileges I'd seen in annuals: sports, girls, cars, dances, and hanging out with buddies.

Curt closes the folder, starts to hand it to Jordan then changes his mind.

"I'll keep this. It has every indication of being an underlying motive for murder. The murders having Miss McIntyre as a pivot cover sixteen years. This letter pertains to events that put our Lieutenant Governor in the cross hairs going back twenty years.

"Maddy Sorals is pushing hard. I got word from the chief last night Sam Sorals murder is now our case as he was pulled out of the river where he drowned.

"Got a class. Talk later."

He takes the folder and goes out the front door. It's raining.

"Who are you going to see?"

"Judge Roach. He is no fan of TT Towbridge and has been a great help in clearing the paperwork of the Dialman estate. Late last evening, before closing he got a zinger.

"A Duncan Abbott has filed papers with the fiscal court, claiming Dialman was mentally unstable, and requesting any will he wrote after his wife died, to be declared null and void.

"Claims, as there is no direct descendent who has come forth to establish claim to the estate, he is the legitimate heir in line to inherit as the only living first cousin on their mother's side.

"He also requests access to all properties which he has been denied by the city police."

"You mean Duncan Abbott as married to TT's niece? As TT's right hand man and shadow?"

"The same."

"What are you going to do?"

"Leg work I expect. Hunting up reputable people who had contact with Mr. Dialman six-months or so prior to his death. I wrote his will over a year ago. He knew exactly what he wanted. I still have my notes from our initial meetings."

"Have fun. Capital City was under water six months ago."

"I also have Elton Fightmaster's sworn deposition signed, witnessed, and notarized by Judge Silas Morgan, stating Dialman had been in communication with him as to his last will and testament by letter and by phone for six months prior to when the will was written."

"Detect TT's hand on the wheel. Law library's close. On the second floor of the Capitol building."

"Thanks for the information. May have to visit it. I see this legal wiggle as an effort to send me on a wild goose chase. Where does it leave you?"

"Behind the eight-ball. No closer to finding the killer than I was when I found Clayton. Need to talk to him to find out why he put the brat in Valley View Children's Home. If I drive down's he up to talking?"

"Sure. Should you leave town?"

"Petra will be safe for a few hours. Desper and Charity are staying in the house. Whoof on guard duty. One of the twins 's napping in Clayton's pad and will be on night duty."

"I was planning to stop by after I see the judge. If it's late I'll take her to lunch."

"She can't possibly get in trouble while I'm gone."

Chapter 23

Whoof gives Jordan his seal of approval when I open the front door. The dog plants himself in front of me and lifts his paw for a hand shake. He has learned Jordan will slip him snacks under the table.

"Let me put my raincoat in the closet so it won't drip on your floor. I'll join you for some of Charity's coffee."

"When she learned you were coming she made pound cake sandwiches. I'll tell her you've arrived."

I hurry down the hall to the kitchen. When I returned Jordan is holding my pea coat."

"Is this yours?"

"Yes, my guardian sent it to me when I learned to sail. It gets cold out on the bay except during mid-summer."

"Do you know where he obtained it?"

"Not exactly. I suspect it was from the Army and Navy Surplus store on Railroad Street. I was in there last week and saw one like it. Why?"

"Curious. It's Coast Guard issue. I have one. Foul weather the wool will shed water like oil on a duck's back."

"True. It's heavy, feels like I'm carrying twenty pound weights on my shoulders."

Charity comes down the hall with her tray piled high with pound cake sandwiches filled with apricot jam.

She likes Jordan. He taught her how they made tea on his ship. It's stronger than coffee with a smoky aroma.

Whoof follows her into the sitting room with his nose in the air and plops down by the chair Jordan uses when he visits.

I'm as bad as the spoiled dog. I can talk to Jordan. He listens to me and understands my fears and confusion. I don't have to pretend with him.

"I like the chaise lounge by the French doors."

"Thank you. It was in the room I'm using for a bedroom. The windows up there face the street. I feel funny when I look out those windows expecting something bad to happen."

"Is it a good idea to have the windows and doors open?"

"Fresh paint smells. You all put dead bolt locks on the doors and gates.

"Jordan, I don't like to be closed in. It frightens me more than standing on a slick deck during a gale.

"You didn't come to listen to my silliness. How can I help you?"

"By being patient. As I told you, we must wait six months to give anyone time to present a claim against the Dialman estate before the final settlement."

"Yes. That's why we drew up a lease with intent to purchase for Charity and Desper."

"Do you play chess?"

"I tried it one night with Evan Blade. It was odd. If I didn't think about it my fingers made the right moves. He asked me where I learned to play. I didn't know."

"Chess was Marcus' game. He taught me and I suspect he taught you.

"What I'm going to tell you is a legal chess game. Opponents block moves till they run out of options.

"A man by the name of Duncan Abbott..."

"I met him the first day I was here. Evan lied about who I was so I told him I was Brenda Burton. The false name just popped out, maybe because I took an instant dislike to him.

"Then one afternoon I was fishing with Wedge Forge. Mr. Towbridge's big cruiser came down the river. A man was watching me through binoculars. Whoof was sitting between us. I still felt creepy. Wedge said the man was Duncan Abbott."

"I see."

He grins and his grey eyes sparkle.

"The next time you go fishing put Anvil on one side and Wedge on the other with Whoof at your feet. They should deter any boogie man."

I laugh. His ability to make me see the humorous side of my fears is one of the things I enjoy about him.

"As hot as it has been, why were you fishing in the afternoon?"

"Wedge said heat-of-the-day fishing wasn't for catching fish, it was for thinking."

"Wise man, Wedge Forge. I need to take time to try it. Back to Abbott.

"He filed papers in the Circuit Court claiming he is the legitimate heir to the Dialman estate. He is also married to Towbridge's other niece."

"Is he the true heir?"

"No. Robert Dialman intended for you to inherit. He specifically named you as the adopted daughter of Marcus Laurence McIntyre."

"Jordan, am I cheating him of his inheritance?"

"No. Blade sees it as a legal maneuver on the part of Towbridge to force you out of the picture. The clincher is your mother's will probated fifteen years ago. She left all her worldly possessions to her husband, which includes a third interest in the Towbridge estate."

"Evan's wrong."

"Why?"

"Mr. Towbridge wouldn't gain anything. In fact he'd lose. If Mr. Dialman's estate goes to Mr. Abbott then he has control of two thirds of the estate. You said Abbott is married to my cousin."

"Bingo. Sis. You opened an interesting angle. I never

thought of it that way. Abbott is sticking a knife in Towbridge's back. Your idea may save me a ton of useless paperwork. Thanks."

He takes a big bite of a sandwich then breaks off a small piece for Whoof.

"Big mutt isn't getting, but a small taste of this. Does Charity make her own jam?"

"She doesn't. She gets homemade items from a grocery in the Bottoms called Grundy's."

"Please. Tell her I want a jar to take to my wife. Do you mind?"

He holds up three sandwiches. Wraps them in a napkin and sticks them in his pocket.

"I'll eat them on the way home. One more thing, may I take you jacket with me? I need to show it to a friend. I'll bring it back."

Jordan breezes out the door with his loot. Whoof is as sad as I am to see him go.

He called me 'Sis' like he meant it.

Wedge and Anvil are friends. They don't make me feel as safe as my big brother.

~ ~ ~

Hate to bother Clayton. Knew bullet tore holes through his gut. Call Mary Forrester from the *Kricket* in Clydesville to let her know I'm coming.

Shocked when I see him. Not good. Color dingy. Clayton's eating baby food. Lost twenty or more pounds. Recovery will be slow. Demands I tell him all that has been happening.

McIntyre was still alive when he found him, but on the way out. Repeated Valley View. Clayton assumed he was telling him where to place Pi. Kept her hidden in a motel for two days while he made arrangements. Matron demanded cash as it was against policy to take paid boarders. Finally agreed to a money order made out to her personally.

He'd agreed to serve as her guardian, if McIntyre was unable a year before his death after he adopted the child.

Clayton got Bradford Roach, now Circuit Court judge, to clear all the legal stuff so the bank could send the money to Florence Emmens for Pi's care. Southern Trust Bank acted as her trustee and Clayton as her guardian. Guardianship officially ended on her twenty-first birthday back in February.

He caught hell for being late getting back to Knox. CO calmed down when he explained the circumstances, then assigned him overseas out of spite.

Didn't know why he moved her to Cardome in secrecy. Had a feeling something wasn't kosher. Figured most of the money was going in the matron's pocket.

Rain follows me down and back. At times it's so hard the two lane road's invisible. Bushed when I pull in stable.

Soaked by the time I get McIntyre's back door open. Try to be quiet.

Whoof's there to greet me. So much for stealth. Give him a rub.

In the fridge Charity has left me a plate of meatloaf, mashed potatoes, peas & onions, rolls, and a side of gravy. Instructions for heating in the microwave printed on warp.

Put it in. Set the timer, head back for milk.

Pi's standing in the laundry room door wearing dotted pajamas and horn rimmed glasses. Holding a gun police style.

"When did you start wearing glasses?"

"Use them for reading late at night. These are bifocals. I wear contacts during the day."

The muzzle doesn't waver. She's steady as a statue in the park.

"Do you ever come by except to eat?"

"Whoof knew."

"Hells bells, scared the billy be-damn out me when he took off like a bat out of hades."

"Put the gun on the counter."

"Why are you here this time of night?"

"Don't have time for hysterics. Tired and hungry."

Microwave buzzer bings. Put the plate on table. Pour a glass of milk and proceed to eat. Ignoring her.

Peaceful silence.

Brat puts the gun down. Stare. Gleaming in the light's a.38 Colt Cobra. Same caliber used in the murders.

Heft it. Nice balance. Point at the back door and eject the cylinder. Dump six steel clad bullets in my hand. Look at the points. No filings. Smell it. Hasn't been fired since it was cleaned.

Newer model than one I have in my safe. Grips are finely hashed walnut.

"Where did you…?"

Damn the brat. While I checked the weapon. She's made a sandwich of half my meatloaf and's calmly drinking my milk.

"Finish your meal."

"What's left of it."

Get a saucy smirk as she chews.

"You didn't have this in your knapsack or case."

"You…you whore hound. You went through my things."

"Of course I did. I'm a detective. Horehound's an herb. Candy made from its syrup's good for coughs and sore throats. Word isn't a swear word."

She bristles like a porcupine. Glaring at me. Stuffs the remainder of the sandwich in her mouth and spits like a scalded kitten.

"Piss poor in my book. You haven't found who killed Mr. McIntyre or my parents."

"Police job. Mine's to keep you alive. Where did you get the gun?"

"Army and Navy Surplus downtown."

"When?"

"Last week."

"Who went with you?"

"I went by myself when you were in the clinic."

"Parked that red and white kitty car in front of the place no doubt. Advertising. Stupid."

Take a hard grip on my temper. Want to grab her and turn her over my knee.

"No, I'm not stupid. Whoof and I walked. He sat outside by the door and wouldn't let anyone in while I was there."

"Proves a point. Dog has more brains than you."

"You listen. I'm sick and tired of being cooped up in an empty house. Can't go fishing without a big lug watching every move. Living in a cell under house arrested like I've committed a crime by existing.

"Watching TV on a tiny black and white screen."

"Dummy, get Desper to buy you a colored model and set it up wherever you want in the house. Make a sitting room upstairs. Have plenty of extra bedrooms."

Take a bite of cooling mashed potatoes to keep from shaking her. Seven people busting butt to protect her from becoming a statistic. All Brat can do's complain.

"I'm a grown woman. I take care of myself. I don't need a bunch of body guards."

"Eat your sandwich."

Let her stew. Finish my supper. Search the fridge for pie. Find it.

"Can you use it?"

"The gun?"

"Yes, Brat. The gun."

"Of course. Juan Torres taught me with a Ruger Bearcat."

"It's a .22. Smaller caliber. Less recoil. Have you fired this pistol?"

"No. Cleaned it."

"Thought so. Handles different. What did you plan to do if you run out of bullets?"

She digs in her pocket and pulls out a thick sock. Dumps a spare cylinder on the counter. Crude, though effective billy club.

"How in the hell are you going to bash some bozo in the head? Carry a stool with you when you go out of the house?"

"You don't listen so I'll repeat it.

"I can take care of myself.

"I've done it for fifteen years without your help."

She glares as she reassembles the Colt with precise movements of a professional.

"We'll see. Tomorrow I'm taking you to the gravel pit where the State Police have a target range. You'll practice until your arms fall off."

"How many ten penny nails will I need to prove to you I know how to handle a firearm?"

Laugh. She remembered what I told her about Abel.

"I'll bring a pound, bent ones don't count."

Snaps the cylinder. Snaps at me.

"Okay."

"Go to bed. Take Whoof with you."

Stomps to the door. Looks back over her shoulder.

"I said okay."

"Would you have shot me?"

"Wounded you a little to let you know I mean business. Only way to get the attention of a boneheaded jackass."

Chapter 24

Towbridge managed to circumnavigate me in spades. Pi and I receive formal invitations to the Governor's Summer Ball at Rolling Acre's Country Club. Command performance which cannot be ignored.

There was no way short of breaking both her legs that I could keep her from attending. Curt will be around as he's elected to head up the security detail, because the ladies drag out all the family jewels and wear them to these affairs. Heist would net a fortune. Even he has to produce the white jacket from mothballs and have it dry cleaned.

Rent a dark blue Buick sedan so it will get lost in the hundreds of like models in the parking lot, to remain in the shadows. Wedge, in full uniform, agrees to be our chauffeur and to stay alert for any problems.

Brat isn't having my careful plans for a low profile evening. When she comes down the stairs all I can do is shutter. Every woman in the ballroom will have her on their hit list within three minutes.

Gown looks like crushed ice. It falls straight to the floor in a long column. Candle light shimmering as she walks. Walks as a harlot on parade, bestowing favors on her hapless subjects. Ditched the wobbly pumps for silver strap sandals with a low heel.

Hair's pulled back under a band of the same material into a mass of curls on the back of her head. She's wearing dark pearl earrings with a ring that matches.

Stunner's a necklace. Fits her like a choke collar dotted with diamonds. In the center, resting in the hallow of her throat's a pear shaped stone that moves as she breathes.

As anticipated, the receiving line's a nightmare. Both TT and his henchman can't take their eyes off the necklace. We finally make it to the door of the ballroom.

Alexandra Stevens, the current State Treasurer, waylays us as we enter. She trades offices back and forth with each election. Has as much or more power than TT. Never lets a stranger go unnoticed.

Tonight she's swinging her shoes with one hand and holding a glass of champagne in the other. Though evening's early it's not her first.

Looks Pi up and down. There isn't anything I can do. I introduce them.

Mrs. Stevens ignores me and rounds on Pi.

"What size shoe do you wear?"

Brat's taken back for a moment by the unexpected question. She smiles without taking offence.

"A four."

"What are you doing at this bordello? You're a lady."

"Thank you. Mr. Blade is extending my education."

Mrs. Stevens squeezes my arm.

"Keep her safe. The cats are on the prowl."

She wanders away whipping those shoes against her side looking for other prey.

Curt greets us wearing a waiter's jacket and a tray with two sparkling glasses of ginger ale. He leads us to reserved seats near the bandstand. Brat takes off to the powder room.

"Don't touch any drinks unless I serve them."

"What's the problem?"

"Ugly rumors. Sticky fingers hit town."

"Good idea. Brat can't hold a drink. Can I help?"

"Keep your eyes open. Abbotts are assigned to your table. She is tipsy."

"Piece your date is wearing, is worth a king's ransom."

Ignore comment about date. Escort duty of the worst kind. Short of having Wedge wreck the rental there was no way to prevent her from coming.

"Costume jewelry."

"Stones are real. White gold with platinum mountings."

"Necklace! Curt, Clara Dialman was wearing a necklace. Stolen after she was dumped according to the police report.

213

TT and Abbott were staring a hole through Petra when we came through the receiving line."

Brat comes back as Abbott plops his wife at the table, not bothering to introduce her, then takes off to talk to Towbridge. They're having an argument.

Pi's trying to table talk with Faith. It's hard going. She's soused.

Faith mumbles, "Haven't…seen Grandmers'…"

She lifts her glass. I see my chance and take it. Move the empty chair next to her with my foot. Glass tumbles from her hand hitting Pi square in the front. Grab her arm.

Whisper as I pull her out of the chair.

"Don't make a scene. She's drunk. Home to change."

Whisk her from the room so fast her feet barely touch the floor.

Outside while we're waiting for the doorman to fetch Wedge I notice a black panel van parked in the shadows near the loading dock. Doesn't have any firm's markings. To help Curt with his problem I use my switch blade on the tires.

If it's legit, a spot of vandalism carries little weight on a big night.

~ ~ ~

"Sorry your evening was a wash out. Change. Hang the dress in the shower. Douse it with cold water. Tomorrow, have Charity take it to the dry cleaners."

She's sniffling. Mascara smeared. Hand her a handkerchief. Woebegone urchin.

"Go on, I'll make coffee."

"I'm hungry."

"Not a bad idea. Pat won't be busy."

"I don't want a burger."

"Okay, I'll call. Tell him to make up some Lobster Cantonese."

"What is it?"

"Ambrosia. Go. Hide the jewels. Curt says those baubles are genuine."

"I know."

"How."

"I took them to Lyons' to be cleaned and sized."

She holds up her hand and counts on her fingers.

"It belonged to my great-great-great-grandmother. I'm the seventh generation to own and wear it."

Dropping her bomb she heads through the laundry room to the stairs.

"Wash your face."

TT knew the minute he saw it. So did Abbott.

~ ~ ~

Between shoveling bits of wild rice, carrots, pork, and chunks of lobster in her mouth with chopsticks, she tells me about the tug-a-war over Dumbo with Whoof.

Forgot to warn her of how he played.

Clara Dialman's jewelry was hidden in the elephant. Who'd be so stupid to hide a fortune in a kid's toy?

TT told me he bought the elephant for her when she was a little tike.

Desperation?

Accident Pi found it.

If Mrs. Dialman was wearing it the night she was killed and it was stolen off her body how in the hell did it end up in the elephant?

When we get back to the house she invites me into the office with a serious look on her face. Motions for me to sit on a sofa in front of the dark green marble fireplace. Goes over to the huge desk at the back of the room.

Look around. Haven't been in here since we polished the floor and put the shelving back. Smells of old money. Pale green walls, light weight silk drapes. Furniture moved. Business efficient. Liveable.

She removes a brown envelope from a drawer and drops it in my lap.

"Read the contents."

It contains two birth certificates and her adoption by Marcus McIntyre papers.

"Who is Brenda Curtis Burton?"

"I don't know. When I left the home to attend high school at Cardome, Matron gave it to me. Said it came with me. It has a birth date February 14, 1957 on it. Thelma Burton Curtis is listed as the mother.

"I searched for two years and located the grave of Thelma. She died when she was eighty-five, five years before I was born. She was a Suffragette. First woman to register to vote in Ono County, Kentucky.

"How did you...?"

She looks at me, as if for a detective I'm a blockhead.

"Library of Congress. Census and voter registration records."

Give her a salute. Lived in Maryland, down the road from the largest vault of information in the world.

"What it has to do with me, I have no idea."

Pick up the Dialman's hospital certificate.

"This 's a forgery."

"What?"

"I searched the Bureau of Vital Statistics. Couldn't locate a record for you as Vivian Phillips Dialman."

"Then I'm not her?"

"Didn't say. Went to Towbridge. After hemming and hawing he told me you were born in New York because of an RH factor blood problem between your parents. Jordan Ames has written for verification, but those responses take time."

"Then the only valid papers are those where Mr. McIntyre adopted me."

217

"Looks like it."

"This isn't a candle lite world where it glitters like the ballroom. I must make my own world, then find a place in it."

Deep statement from the brat who's wearing a sailor's hat balanced on a party hair do. Her mouth's grim with determination. She wants something McIntyre and Dialman's money combined can't give her.

She wants to belong.

Don't have the courage to tell her it won't happen, not in this lifetime.

"Sounds like common sense."

"Don't you wonder what people think of you?"

"No, I let them wonder what I think of them."

"Evan, who am I?"

Chapter 25

Abbott's waiting with TT's car outside my place. His grand standing as a Bogart tough guy makes me want to belt him in the kisser. Expected the command summons.

His Burma Shave's enough to gag a mule. Smells like bad medicine.

When we get out of the car, he starts to take my arm. Bat it away like his hand's a fly. Look down at him. Snarl.

"Don't touch. You don't want to eat through a straw."

We make it to TT's office in silence. Before Abbott closes the door his master shouts.

"Where did she get the necklace?"

"You gave it to her."

"I did no such thing. It was my great-grandmother's. She wore it to a ball at the White House, when she danced with Benjamin Harrison in 1890. My grandfather added the five caret teardrop diamond for my grandmother on their fiftieth wedding anniversary. That necklace is a valuable family heirloom."

"Yes, you did. You told me yourself – you gave her the elephant."

Stares at me with cold blue eyes that indicate I've left planet earth.

Enjoying jerking his chain. Time to end the game. Tell him about the tug-a-war with Whoof. How Pi found the jewelry.

He collapses in his chair, elbows propped on his desk, and his hands holding the sides of his head, as if he has a violent headache.

"Earrings and ring?"

"Same. Diamond studs, rope of pearls, and other pieces."

"I brought the pearls back from Rome when I was in the Army as loose balls in my pocket. Black market. People sold anything for American dollars. Had Lyons make them up for Clara as a wedding present. Robert gave her the studs for an anniversary present."

He's rambling. Hasn't asked himself the important questions.

"It's not possible they were in the elephant."

"Yes. According to Miss McIntyre, a gardener kept that stuffed toy in his shed while she lived at the children's home. Gave it to her as she was leaving. Blind luck it wasn't thrown in the trash.

"Your sister was wearing them the night she died. They were ripped from her body. No description in the police report.

"You gave me the death scene photos. Had some blown up. Shoe on her left foot had a broken heel. You told me she broke her heel. Ear lobes torn. Cuts on her neck, but no blood near the wounds.

"Details you've been keeping from me. Why the secrecy?"

"I didn't see her until the funeral. Robert didn't mention them. I assumed he had Clara's jewelry in his safety deposit box for Vivian."

"Lockbox? Ames didn't list a box on his inventory of Dialman's estate."

"Blade, every family has a one in a bank vault. You don't know women. They don't keep family pieces at home. It's too dangerous. They trot them out for formal occasions to impress other women. You saw it last night.

"Thanks to Lieutenant Colton's fast thinking, this morning they're back in the bank."

"What's back in the bank?"

"Jewelry. Last night."

"What happened last night?"

"You were there."

"No, we left early. Faith dumped her drink on Miss McIntyre while Abbott was talking to you. Took her home to change. Couldn't come back…no spare evening gown."

Abbott hadn't told him we were absent when the dinner began. What else does he keep from TT?

"Thieves dressed as waiters snatched jewelry the women were wearing. When they got to their van with the spoils, the Lieutenant had flatten their tires and had them surrounded.

"No embarrassment for the club. The State Police returned the stolen items to their owners. The ball continued on schedule despite the unpleasant interruption.

"Smart man, the Lieutenant. Knows how to keep ugly stuff quiet until the governor can prepare a statement. I've recommended to the chief he be given a promotion."

Good for Curt. Pay raise should help cover his new expenses. Ex didn't leave him much when she took off.

Local gossips will keep the story buzzing for weeks. Didn't guess wrong.

Don't want TT asking questions I can't answer. This isn't getting me to the truth. Throw him a zinger to get back on track.

"You believed Dialman killed your sister."

His face's bleak. He nods.

"Couldn't prove it because he was with you. What changed a fifteen year vendetta?"

"His murder."

"Figures. Told you when I took this case I didn't want it. Your golden rule's step on toes the way you don't want someone to step on yours.

"Not one of your 'on-demand' boys. Right now all I have about your sister's murder are a bunch of bits and pieces which don't add up."

"You've been working for weeks."

"Told you what I've learned. Big questions?"

"Like what?"

TT's on the verge of losing his temper. Voice sounds like I'm talking to myself.

"Times. You and Dialman both stated he arrived at the reception about 6:45. State Crime Lab gives time of death near eight PM or later. She'd been physically beaten. No evidence found in the Dialman home. Wearing shoe with broken heel which says she never made it back to the house after Dialman drove off. Where was she for one and a half to two hours before she was killed?"

"How?"

"Thunderation. Did you flunk math? You've had those reports for fifteen years."

"Never thought."

"Obviously. While we're on simple. Photos showed the body in a curled position. It had to have been that way for two to three hours because her body fluids had settled to her left side. My guess 's her body was stashed in the trunk of a car, soon after she was killed, for a period of time before being dumped."

"The police never told me any of this."

"What did they have back then? Bunch of dodo birds? Johnson would have spotted what I've told you in less than five minutes."

His eyes close to tight squints. Blue pin-point glare bores into me. Heads are going to roll. Mine along with them, so I'd better force the truth out of him before he delivers sentence. Pi's life depends on it.

Clayton Forrester told me McIntyre was dying, but not dead when he found him. Struggling to talk and clearly said Valley View. He assumed he was giving him instructions about the child. Looked it up in a phone book and found Valley View Children's Home.

After the police left he made arrangements for her shelter. He was two days over due at Fort Knox.

Located an old Army buddy who was a gardener to watch over her while he was overseas.

His job made it impossible for him to be on the scene. Continued to locate military contacts, to keep an eye pealed wherever Petra lived. They reported to him. George Stanopolis taught her to drive.

Damn. The egghead school in Maryland wasn't a whim. Clayton deliberately stashed her where his friends were stationed close by to protect her.

Later learned the gardener was fished out of a pond a week after he removed Petra from the home. The man had been in a fight.

"Why the song and dance about not knowing where Petra was after your sister died?"

"I didn't."

"Towbridge, that's impossible. You're chairman of the Board of Trustees of the Valley View Children's Home."

"Yes. Honorary. Great-great-grandfather built the original log structure because 'movers' kept dropping unwanted children off at the farm gates. Had no place to put them. Older children took care of the younger ones. Gave them jobs on the farm when they were old enough to help."

Bragging like the old man performed a benevolent social duty instead of acquiring free labor. Stomach churns.

"Pass it on the way in from the farm, but haven't been on the place more than three times since my brother died. Mother took care of the ribbon-cutting duties for the family. My name is on dozens of boards. I don't even know the names of all of them."

Anger at his blind arrogance destroys my common sense.

"Petra McIntyre was a paid boarder at the home for seven years. You want me to believe you never saw your own niece?

"Go see your doctor. You're a class "A" candidate for a hemorrhoidal study."

225

Spin to the door. Abbott opens it. Hides a grin.

Hear brushing sound of fabric against fabric.

Duck.

Abbott takes the hit from a paperweight aimed at my head.

Chapter 26

Meet Curt for breakfast. Sit in a booth where we can see doors and parking lot. Little on the street at five in the morning. Have the place to ourselves.

Waitress knows what we want, how we like it. Coffee's on the table along with the *Capital Advocate* when I join him. He's working the crossword puzzle. Gives a grunt of greeting without looking. No need for social niceties before the sun peeks over the yardarm.

Pick up the first section to scan the headlines until my meal arrives.

"Gave the recruits a group assignment. They were to pull, cull, and match anything we had on dead or missing children, Fog Landing, river crimes, going back twenty-five years.

"Chief will have a coronary when he sees the man hours they logged. Our old files are a mess or missing.

"It wasn't my idea. When they weren't coming up with diddly they pooled ideas. Then, went out in civies and combed old newspaper files in surrounding counties, plus those that touch the river. It was a back breaker of a job, but the morgues of those local papers yielded the most information.

"One is a business major who studied accounting. He purchased a wide tablet from an office supply store and started filling in columns with notes."

I watch a couple of guys come in and take seats at the counter with their backs to our booth. I've see one somewhere before, but his face isn't ringing a bell.

Curt talks in a soft voice to cover his excitement. His rookies have uncovered something he's keeping under wraps. It's big and ugly.

"We have enough information, but no solid evidence to put Barge Jack Dawson and his gang of scum, away for the rest of their unnatural born lives. He is no spring chicken."

"Who's Barge Jack Dawson?"

"River legend for corruption who has operated out of Fog Landing for decades. Never been able to touch him."

"What about Rusty? He's a witness."

"No. Same situation as here. I won't put him in danger. Rusty doesn't trust me as it is. I may be his blood uncle, proven on paper, but I'm still a fuzz."

Curt smiles for the first time since we started eating.

"Anvil helped him rig a CB radio station in the trailer. Truckers use them. He listens in on channel 19 and chats with them. Calls me at night, gave me the handle of 'Captain.' Has one lined up for you, 'Gumshoe.' His is 'Harbor Master.'"

Rusty's leeriness of the law doesn't extend to his uncle. Kid's holding on with all his might to a two-way street.

"Tell Harbor Master to keep mum as to home dock."

Place's filling up with early traffic. Two coffee drinkers sitting at the counter are straining their ears to catch every word. Dart my eyes back and forth. Curt takes notice.

"Rumors flying the oldest profession's working rest stops out of pickups with camper shells. Grinders bark channel 19. Roll their marks and move on. Suckers wake up in their rig with a mickey headache and no cush."

Curt laughs out loud. Then whispers, "Will do. I'll pass your message, in English, to the guys up north. I75 is their turf."

Make a mental note to get a CB for the truck. Don't have to have a license, as required for a shortwave radio. Avoid anything that pins me to a location, which can be traced if one hunts hard enough.

Curt continues the story in a low tone. Listeners give up and move around the counter to greener pastures. Now that I can see their faces, one's a reporter for the *Advocate*, but I can't remember his name.

"On the way down to the lake Rusty filled me in on how he managed to get back to Capital City from Fog Landing.

"His step-father, Foreman Otis is a drunk. He sold him to that notorious foul river character.

"Dawson has been in and out of jails going back to Prohibition. No court has been able to nail him to send him up the river. Missing witnesses, bad memories, or hung juries.

"You know the score.

"Dawson resold Rusty to a white slave trader to be ship to New Orleans, to feed that cesspool of purveyors of young boys for prostitution.

"He overheard Dawson make the sale. When they unlocked the hole were he was held he fought. Took one hell of a beating.

His captors thought he was out. When they brought him up for the transfer he broke loose and dived in the river. Climbed out up stream into a sewage pipe and hid. Crawled through the sludge to a road.

"Middle of the night. Found a locked gas station/diner. Hid in the dumpster. Scared off some raccoons who'd dug out the remains of a burger. Ate it. Slept in a stall in the ladies' restroom.

"Managed to climb into the back of cattle truck loaded with feeder calves heading to the stockyards. Drop out somewhere above your place. Passed out in a ditch. The terrier found him and Sam carried him to the shelter.

"Came to as Sam was pulling off his filthy jeans. Fought him. He was too weak to put up much resistance. Sam hauled him up and shoved him in the shower. Then put a bowl of chili on a table, in the shower room and left him alone."

Eaten Sam's chili. Will grow hair on your chest. He used it to sober up drunks.

"Talking too much. Worst thing about this job. I don't have anyone to bounce ideas off. Chief is a by-the-book officer. If it isn't printed in regulations he loses his hearing."

Curt left his procedure manuals on the plane when he landed in 'Nam. We made it home, which's what counts at roll call.

"Anyway, to make a long story short, Sam gave him clean clothes, a comic book, and pointed to a bunk. You came in. He fell asleep. You know the rest."

Pride Curt has for his nephew rings in his voice. Admiration for Rusty's courage. Weird twist of fate lead the kid to the one man who has spent a lifetime protecting his men.

When they first met, Anvil and Wedge had been determined to put him in the brig after his slight of hand transfer of them to his platoon. Now they'll walk over the coals of hell to carry out his orders.

Curt looks over my shoulder and frowns. Turn my head to see who has his attention. TT, followed by Abbott is coming in the back door on their way to the private dining room. TT nods like he's giving an audience to humble supplicates.

Start to get up. I know somewhere in this foul mess he has his dirty paws. Everything points to him, no matter how loud he proclaims his innocence.

Curt grips my arm. He knows I'm primed to deck the son-of-a-bitch as a courtesy.

"No. Leave it. Don't let your temper blow our case."

Heat of anger rages. Hear his voice from beyond the flames.

Curt pushes a cup of coffee in front of me. Pries my fingers apart. Pokes the cup in my hand.

Pick it up. Wobbles so hard the brew sloshes out into the saucer. Drink the scalding coffee to get a grip. Sizzles my mouth.

"You can't touch him. Not under any circumstances. That is an order, my friend."

"Why not?"

"Hell's bells, Evan. What is TT's full name?"

"Thornton Thomas Towbridge."

"Who reared you?"

"Aloysius Thornton."

"Who was your great-uncle. Are you blind?"

"You're trying to tell me, we're some kind of kin?"

"Not only that blockhead, but according to my Uncle Ben, who knows how those things work, you're his legal heir after his nieces."

Ben Colton isn't one to make a mistake on relationships. He's a professional genealogist. People pay him to research their ancestry.

Gulp another slug of coffee to clear the haze of anger.

"Does he know?"

"Sure. TT Towbridge knows every member of his family. He keeps track of them. It's a hobby with him."

"The bastard. Thanks for stopping me from making a bad move."

"True. He knows he has you tied in a corner any time he wants to pull the cord."

"Curt, I don't give a damn about being his heir."

"I know you don't, but Martin Stokes, the reporter for the *Advocate* would have a field day with a brawl between you and TT. Even if he has no idea what is behind it."

"I'll dig in every garbage pit I can find until I can prove he's guilty or innocent. If guilty, I'll destroy him."

"If he proves to be the lynch pin in this filthy mess I will lend you the sword and back you to the hilt. Until then, smile, be polite, and forget we ever had this conversation."

Chapter 27

" Where's Ames?"

It would be pleasant if for once Blade asked 'How are you, Petra?' or even said, 'Hello, nice morning.' Not him.

He never knocks. Comes in the back door. Stands there, pouring himself a cup of coffee, like he owns the place and barking questions.

"I don't know."

"Called. Asked me to meet him here."

For all his rough exterior, I'm glad to see him.

Last night I used the opera glasses to peer across the street. I'd polished the case with toothpaste and cleaned the lenses. It shines and the stones in the flowers glitter. Holding it to my eyes felt familiar, but I had to adjust them to fit my wider face.

Instantly, I found the window of Charity's house where Clayton set up a surveillance room for this house. There were no lights. Their car was in the garage. The dark driveway was shadowed by the house. I kept looking for a strange car though I knew they'd gone to bed.

There was the shadow of a man in front of my house near the street light. It wasn't bulky enough to be Wedge. Before I located him his shadow disappeared.

Whoof was restless. He kept going to the window and looking out. His nails clicking on the floor kept me awake. I took him to the back bedroom opening out to the porch. We slept there.

The twins keep a thermos of coffee and a sack of sandwiches on the porch for when they take a break. I feel safer in that bedroom knowing one of them is outside.

The door bell rings. Jordan. He's my brother, yet he is polite and doesn't presume. He comes to the front door and rings the bell.

"I'll get it."

Billy Bejaysus, the arrogant wharf rat assumes he is the master of the house. Won't let me answer my own door.

Whoof follows him. I trail behind like a lost orphan.

Jordan enters, followed by a stranger. A small man dressed in a plaid sports shirt over a stark white t-shirt, crisp starched khakis, and leather moccasins. The man is older than Jordan and very shy. He barely nods his head, then studies me from under bushy eyebrows from light brown eyes.

Jordan has on cowboy boots with his suit, so this is a social visit. When he comes as my lawyer he wears dress shoes. He holds my pea coat on his right arm with his briefcase in his left hand. His eyes dance like he holds the secret to the universe.

"Petra, I brought someone you need to meet. Let's go in the parlor and I'll make the proper introductions. Evan, please join us."

Strangely, Jordan appears to be nervous. The way he invites Blade to join us voices a plea for backup.

We're standing in the middle of the room like scattered chess pieces on a board, after an abandoned game.

Jordan takes my hand and gives it a squeeze.

"Petra Isolta McIntyre, I want you to meet a former shipmate of mine, Innis Morgan."

Mr. Morgan takes my hand and holds it for a moment. I can feel the rough scars from shucking oysters. He is from the bay, the feel is unmistakable.

I smile in recognition of the scars.

"Pleased to meet you, ma'am."

His soft rolling voice tumbles through my memory. I've heard the unique sound hundreds of times from the trawlers putting into the docks to sell their catch.

"The islands near Charleston."

"Yes, ma'am. Seamew."

Whoof bumps between us, extending his paw to be shaken, which Mr. Morgan does with enthusiasm.

Jordan puts his briefcase on the coffee table and drops the coat beside his chair. A sweep of his hand indicates Mr.

Morgan take the chair beside him. Evan and I are waved to the love seat.

Evan places his arm across the back in a possessive gesture. I can feel the heat from it on my neck. Whoof plants his hot body between us and lays down.

Charity in a blaze of color, bustles through the door carrying a the rattan tray loaded with a stoneware pot and mugs.

"Please, don't get up."

It's like she is expecting this to be a kaffee-kiatsch not worthy of the silver service.

"Help yourself."

Jordan moves his briefcase. She puts the tray on the coffee table and whirls from the room.

I fill the mugs and pass them around. Curious as to Charity's behavior.

"Sis, I'm going to tell you about Innis Morgan and then he can tell you his story in his own words.

"I've known him for more years than either of us want to count. He was the cook on our patrol boat. He hit a bad patch and was arrested, then convicted for a crime he did not commit. Eventually, his sentence was rescinded when he was proven innocent and he received a full pardon.

"Silas Morgan of Ono County, is his uncle. Judge Morgan has served as our Circuit Court Judge for many years.

"After his father died, Innis came to Ono County. He helped me restore my grandparents home, found a new wife, and they have a daughter.

"Listen carefully to what he has to say. The principals in his story are dead. Clayton Forrester rushed up here to contact you and to discover if he could help Innis with a search he has conducted for over twenty years. He was shot before he could talk to you."

I look at Mr. Morgan. He is watching me from eyes I see every morning in the mirror, more amber than brown. I ease back against the settee. Evan's hand rests on my shoulder.

My hands tremble. I clasp them hard, my nails making circles in my palms. I'm afraid to listen, but lean forward as if my life depends on it.

Mr. Morgan bends over and picks up my coat. He turns it inside out.

"Jordan tells me Clayton Forrester sent you this coat when you were in college. Do you know where he got it?"

"No. I assumed he bought it at the Army and Navy Surplus store."

"He didn't. He found it in the same place Jordan found it, in a closet of this house.

"The coat belonged to me. See, here is my name 'I. Morgan' on the label on the inside pocket, like all Coast Guard jackets are marked."

He holds out the coat to me. I'd worn the coat the four years I'd spent in college. The name on the label meant nothing to me as I'd assumed Clayton had picked it up in a used clothing store. I drop it like I'm holding a red-hot branding iron.

He turns it out to a side seam and holds it up for me to see. I'd never noticed the small darn. In very fine stitches a small tear had been embroidered with the intertwined initials I. M. There isn't anything I can say, my beloved pea coat belongs to this man.

I push it away toward him. A brief shadow of hurt crosses his face.

"The initials don't stand for Innis Morgan. My first wife's name was Martha. The first time I was home on leave after entering the service I caught my jacket on a nail in the barn and snagged it. My wife darned it so it wouldn't show...she was handy with a needle and intertwined our initials."

"Keep it. I know it belongs to you. I would have returned it if I'd known."

"I know you would. May I tell you about the night Martha was murdered?"

Jordan hasn't said a word. Evan's hand is gripping my arm. I don't want to hear his story, yet I know I must.

"Yes."

"I met a man by the name of Algin Carstairs in a bar in Charleston where I was celebrating my daughter's christening. I was half drunk. He mentioned he knew Silas Morgan, who is my uncle.

"I invited him out to the island to dine with my family. Wanted to show off my daughter.

"He played with her. Dangled his watch chain for her to bat back and forth. We ran out of beer. I left to go back across the causeway to obtain a fresh supply."

Mr. Morgan stops talking. He traces the embroidered initials with a gentle finger and clears his throat before taking a drink of coffee.

Charity comes back into the room, breaking the tension gripping me. She places a plate of chicken salad sandwiches on the table. Picks up the coffee jug, looks at Jordan who nods and retreats.

Using the napkins on the tray I hand everyone a sandwich. I take my time being careful to place them in a precise position. The men accept them.

I know they aren't the least interested in eating. I know I'm dithering, putting off hearing the rest of Mr. Morgan's story.

He said his first wife was murdered.

I want to scream no…no. My parents were murdered. My adoptive father was murdered. Matron was murdered. Evan's friend was murdered.

Will it ever stop?

"Sis, are you okay? You're staring into space."

Jordan's question brings me back to myself. I wanted to run away. Somewhere no one will ever find me.

"Huh. Yes, I'm sorry. I was wool gathering for a moment. Please continue, Mr. Morgan."

"Are you sure, miss?"

The deep concern in his rolling voice is stronger than the sound of the ocean pounding a deserted beach.

I reach out and take his scar roughened hand, which he grasps in a firm clasp.

"There isn't much more I have to tell."

"Please finish."

"When I got back they were gone: Carstairs, my wife, and my daughter. My father was unconscious on the floor inside the door. The doctors at the hospital said he'd ingested a hallucinogenic drug.

"Come daylight a neighbor found Martha on the beach. She was dead. Her neck was broken. My daughter and this ole pea coat were nowhere to be found.

"No one believed my story. I served time in prison. For many years I figured Carstairs had killed her.

"My father never recovered his right mind. Until the day he died he was haunted by Martha. Told anyone who'd listen to him she was his wife. Didn't know me.

"Towards the end he kept talking like she was in the room. I understood. He'd took a fit and killed her. He hated the idea she had a slave for an ancestor. She was more

241

Indian than nigger with bits of others thrown in, like it always is when generations of people live by the ocean.

"Happened way back after the fighting. Plantation owner married his housekeeper in a Christian ceremony. He did right by his children out of her."

I blanch. The man who pushed me down the stairs called me a nigger.

"Sherman gave the islands to the slaves. Never understood – few islanders were slaves in the first place.

"Excuse me, miss. I got off on a trail. It isn't important."

Tears run down Mr. Morgan's face. He turns his head away and stares out the French doors at the garden.

"Sis, Clayton and I've put together a summary as to what may have happened the night Innis' life and family were destroyed. It's supported by the evidence we have.

"You are the missing daughter."

"What?"

My foot starts shaking like a doctor is testing my reflexes. I shove it under Whoof. He doesn't protest.

"I…I am Mr. Morgan's daughter?"

"Yes, we believe it to be so and a blood test can prove it."

"But…"

Evan nudges me.

"Brat, listen to what they have to say, because it could answer a multitude of questions I've uncovered."

I'm too emotionally exhausted to do more than shake my head in denial.

"Legally, you are Petra Isolta McIntyre. You were officially adopted by Marcus Laurence McIntyre. He was married to my mother, so we are, for better or worse brother and sister.

"Algin Carstairs is dead. He supported himself after a failed university teaching career in the black market baby trade."

Jordan opens his brief case and takes out a photostat and a yellowing certificate.

"This is the christening certificate dated February 24, 1958 for Marie Louise Morgan, who was born to Martha Townsend Morgan and Innis Lewis Morgan, on February 14, 1958. With this document I was able to obtain a photostatic copy from the registry of live births, from South Carolina."

He hands them to me. They flutter as ashes in the wind. I study each and drop them in my lap. All my adult life I've searched to discover who I am.

Now, I find it hard to accept.

"Sis, Algin Carstairs must have wrapped you in Innis' jacket and fled back to Kentucky, where he had a ready market for a newborn.

"Evan told me you have a certificate showing the name Brenda Curtis Burton. Would you mind getting it for me?"

I flee. I run across the hall, almost bumping into Charity, who is listening by the door. She follows me into the library, takes one look at my face and shakes her finger at me.

"You've had a shock. Get those papers and go back in there with your fangs polished."

I laugh though it's near hysteria. Take a firm grip on my chaotic emotions and follow her orders.

~ ~ ~

I hand the envelope containing the conflicting certificates to Jordan. Then resume my seat by Evan, holding my spine erect as the sisters taught me: my feet crossed, and my hands curled in my lap.

He studies the hospital certificates for Brenda and Vivian. Turns them over and examines the back.

"Evan, come over to the doors for a minute and hold these up to the light."

Mr. Morgan and I hang in suspenseful silence, almost afraid to breathe while we watch them. I pick up my mug. The coffee is cold.

Charity floats into the room with the stone jug. Starts back to the door.

"Sit down. You've been listening anyway."

"How?"

"Your shadow."

"Petra, stop feeding Whoof. Chicken salad has onions."

I look down. Whoof has been sneaking nibbles of the sandwich I hold in my left hand. He takes the rest of it and tosses his head at Evan.

Mr. Morgan laughs and we relax.

"Sis, these are both forgeries. Excellent work by two different people that will pass the examination of a casual glance.

"This is pure speculation on my part, but I'd say Carstairs couldn't afford, for obvious reasons, to sell you under your real name. So he concocted the Brenda Curtis Burton certificate.

"Those are common Ono County names no one would question and passed you off to the Dialmans as illegitimate. The journeyman neglected one item. The year you were born. On the certificate it says 1957, instead of 1958.

"Second guessing is dangerous. Carstairs may have used a certificate from a previous sale. He also had a confederate, so the paper may have come from the same source.

"The Dialmans were desperate enough for a child to purchase one on the black market. They too had a problem. A matter of what is known as progenitor or direct line of descent. It's a tradition never incorporated into American law, but widely practiced in England, Europe, and by custom especially among families in the American South. It means all properties and possessions go directly to the oldest surviving male heir.

"Siblings, illegitimate children, and adoptions are not included in the inheritance. Clara Dialman's parents changed the custom and left their estate to their three legal children to be held jointly.

"It's impossible to ascertain the motives of the decreased. I'd guess this was behind the elaborate subterfuge of your acquisition by the Dialmans. We simply don't know, but you were never formally adopted as Vivian Phillips Dialman."

"Does what you're telling me mean Mr. Towbridge is not my uncle?"

"Yes, at least not in any blood sense, except with Dialman leaving his possessions to you, there is a legal connection. You still own one-third of the Towbridge's family holdings.

"The claim by Duncan Abbott against the estate, to prove Mr. Dialman was incompetent, was withdrawn. One reason being Elton Fightmaster's deposition. More importantly, Mr. Dialman had lunch with Judge Roach at the county club to discuss rumors of TT Towbridge making a run for the governorship, the day before he was murdered.

"When Towbridge was contacted by Judge Roach, he avowed any knowledge of Abbott's claim or actions. He promised the Judge the matter would be resolved. Abbott withdrew his claim the same afternoon.

"The McIntyre adoption is valid as I told you. Even with it, there are discrepancies which can not be explained. The adoption papers filed in Ono County are dated March 23,

1961, which would have made you three years old at the time.

"The problem is, it was before my mother died. I visited as often as I could get leave while she was ill. You were not present. Nor was there any mention of you. My mother died on July 28, 1963. Clara Dialman was murdered in June of 1964.

"You were here in October of 1964 when I stayed for ten days. Whenever we took you any place outside the garden we always left through the garage. Marcus would take us out-of-town for dinner or to a movie.

"Marcus filed your adoption papers here in Ridgeway County on December 7, 1964. The same day Clara Dialman's estate was finalized and released by the court.

"He was murdered on December 8, 1964. The day after he filed those papers. He was doing his best to protect you from something or someone.

"How and when Marcus acquired the pea coat is anybody's guess. Clayton found it in a closet upstairs and moved it down because the hall closet is cedar lined to keep moths at bay. A sensible gesture on his part to protect wool.

"Clayton was still in the Army when he discovered the murder. The bag of jewelry was in his pocket. Clayton is the person who hid them in the body of your stuffed elephant. He kept his promise to Marcus to see you safe and planted friends near you to stand in for him.

"It was the best he could do given the circumstances of his work and assignments. For a little girl to be so alone for so long, must have been pure hell. We have a rough idea of what you've endured, but can never know what it cost."

"Jordan, I'm a grown up woman. It was a long time ago. Right now I'm overwhelmed and confused.

"If what you and Mr. Morgan are saying is true. I was four different people, before I was five years old.

"Mr. Morgan, I don't mean to be rude…"

"No, miss. You aren't rude. We've laid a ton of bad stuff on you. But please, call me Innis."

I take his hand and hold it tight.

"As I started to say I need to think. To sort everything out in my own mind.

"Petra McIntyre has been my name for as far back as I can remember. My friends call me, Pi."

Chapter 28

Demands of this case have kept me away from my place.

Don't lie to yourself, Blade. Running as hard as Brat.

Barren without Sam or Yippi barking at ants. Smells of mold where crawl space has been closed for days.

Tried dozens of ways of combining notes. Never managed to get the hang of it. Spent more time fixing a method than compiling facts.

Maddy's scrounging solved the problem. Old school was slated for demolition. Found a long slate blackboard complete with chalk tray and felt erasers. Her guys removed it intact and mounted it along one wall of my inner office. Gave me a carton of chalk for Christmas.

Works with plenty of space to add notes at the side of a column. See an entire case laid out from my desk. Chair rolls over to add or erase bits I don't see as relevant. Miscellaneous junk I add on a single section at the end. Use colored chalk to make arrow connections between the columns.

Print as Ames does. Easier to read across the room. Said he learned when he tried engineering on for a profession. I learned at a blackboard, much like this one, in a one-room school near the river.

Lay out notebooks, evidence folders, daily summaries, and go to work at the board. Build the case.

Phone rings. Look at my watch. Been at it for three hours. Lost track of time. Curt asks if I've eaten. Volunteers to stop by Bihn's on his way out.

Light smudge pots to ward off the mosquitoes and no-see-ems. Putting a couple of Falls Cities on the spool table when he pulls around the corner of the warehouse.

He's whipped. Leaves jacket and tie in the car. Shirt sleeves rolled. Collar open. Removes his shoulder holster and puts it on the bench beside him.

Works his shoulders to get kinks out.

"Some place. Hard to find. Was only out this way the one time."

"Suits me."

Open our burgers and fries. He dips a fry in a tub of ketchup. Looks at it. Drops it back in the box. Picks up the burger. Takes a small bite. Chews. Reaches for the beer.

"Got Ale 8's if you're still on duty."

"If you've got a spare bed I'll hide out where reporters can't find me."

"Whole bunk house. Rough day?"

"One I never want to relive."

Talk when he's ready. We eat and watch two runabouts dart down the river to home ports.

Bats that roost on the rafters of the garage area of the warehouse swoop out through gathering dusk. Cicadas chatter. Bull frogs grunt. Fish, snatching flies, splash in the river.

Curt kills the beer. Get him a second which he nurses, turning the can round and round in the wet circle on the table.

"Is it safe to take a swim?"

"River's muddy."

"Be clean after what I've seen."

He starts stripping down to his skivvies.

"How long has it been since we went skinny dipping in the river?"

"Couple of life times."

"Last one in is a rotten egg!"

Belly-flops sting worse than bees. Have no more business being in the river with night coming on than we did as kids. Feels good to float watching stars appear.

Dripping, shaking, and carrying his side arm I take him down to Sam's side. Find the spare key. Flip the light.

"Shower's through there. Everything you need in big cabinet by the door."

Find two pair of sweats with a reasonable fit and flip flops. Dig in the freezer for sweet rolls.

"Clean clothes on a cot. Meet you back at the spool."

~ ~ ~

Watch him come down the walk. Slinking like a mangy hound. Bends to peer into the crawl space.

Hand him a mug of coffee laced with sugar and three large sweet rolls. Digs in like he hasn't eaten in twenty-four hours.

"Sam's place?"

"Yeah."

"Where did all the stuff come from? More soap than we had in 'Nam."

"Maddy supplies it with left overs her people cull when they clean hotel and motels rooms."

"Low overhead."

"Never charged. Left a big mayo jar on counter. If a guy had it he left a donation. If he was short Sam gave him a loan. Same with the clothes. Supplies got cleaned out after the flood. National Guard took up a collection to restock. Didn't ask questions as to source."

"Midnight requisition."

Night folds around us. Faces hidden in shadows. Silence expressing trust.

"Raided Valley View Children's Home. We saw stuff in 'Nam we'll never forget."

Curt has a vice grip on my arm. Holding on to keep from coming apart.

"Since the Emmens woman retired two months ago there hasn't been a matron or an adult on the place. Two boys fifteen or so running it as a brothel for perverts – to buy food. They know no other way of living.

"We have them in custody, but don't know what in the hell to do with them. They clammed up tighter than a barrel of fresh whiskey. Doctors suspect they've been sexually violated for most of their lives.

"Using the younger kids as their merchandise. One girl with no arms isn't yet three.

"Gained a new respect for Children's Services. They helped us interview each child. Our uniforms scared the hell out of those kids. Try to get near them and they started screaming.

"CS found emergency shelters for them in clinics. Tonight a half dozen are in various hospitals under observation. Eighteen in all. Some didn't know their own names. All we could do was assigned them numbers to keep track.

"Found two small boys chained to beds. Lying in filth. It took two officers to hold one until he understood we weren't going to hurt him. He was bleeding from the rectum."

Rocked on his foundations. I'm not far behind. Seeing the horror through his eyes.

"Two girls in the Miner's to be cleaned out from the waist down because of a gonorrhea infection. They're near the same age as Miss McIntyre was when she lived there…less than five.

"No records. What passed for an office emptied. No one knows where those kids came from. A couple are severely mentally retarded. One suffers from Down Syndrome. Another has twisted limbs, broken and never set at some point. Throw away human beings I'm sworn to protect."

His words come slow and halting. Each kid's a spike driven through his heart.

"One little girl kept talking about her friend who never came back from 'the room.' We found 'the room' at the head of the stairs, done up with Disney characters. Big heart shaped bed. Mattress stained on both sides with blood.

"Tomorrow we'll begin searching for a burial ground. Anybody's guess what we'll find.

"Evan, I found myself glad Peter Faulks died. No telling how long this has been going on. I'll kill the bastards if I ever get my hands on them."

Sees Rusty teetering on the brink of a chasm, into which he could have fallen if he hadn't had the guts to cut and run.

"Towbridge and Abbott arrived followed by a string of reporters. Neighbor saw our cars and called him. Obscene circus.

"TT was livid. Turned on Abbott accusing him for allowing this disaster to his family trust. Abbott screaming at him denying any knowledge. Declaring the place was always clean when he made his weekly inspections.

"Downy kid ran up to Abbott, started rubbing his pants at his crotch saying 'treat, treat.' Abbott was terrified of him and lost it. Started to slap him. TT blocked his arm. Tried to pick up the child. Kid bit him.

"Chief, the coward, delegated me to calm him down, and get him and his entourage out of there while he handled the press. This is one that can't be glossed over and hidden on the back pages."

~ ~ ~

Nightjar streaks across the river. Shrill screech stringing behind his wake. Screams of pain I'd heard echoing Pi's soul reflect through Curt's narration. Lost kids, victims of greed, sold to the highest bidder to be used and discarded.

We're lost in our own thoughts of those we know, love, and hope to save.

Bobbi Vance, my foster daughter. Both parents dead. No next of kin willing to step up to the plate.

Rusty Russell, Curt's nephew. Scrappy tiger whose personal habits spell early love and care.

Petra McIntyre, adored, stolen, and sold. Pitched from pillar to post to foster the rancid ambitions of others.

Dropped in a vicious world where her unique racial heritage and an absentee guardian protected her.

Morgan's a sincere okay guy. Don't know what kind of reception he expected. It wasn't what he got. Brat became stiff and formal. Shook hands with each of us as if we were strangers she'd just met. Called Whoof to heel and marched from the room.

Charity followed them with her hands fluttering behind her back.

Morgan never took his eyes off Brat. Stood tall on salute until they were gone.

Jordan invited me to join them for lunch at Serafini before they headed back. I opted to police the coffee table of cold coffee and stale sandwiches. Munched a couple in the kitchen while cleaning up.

Charity didn't return. Stalled leaving, as long as I could find an excuse. Brat was taking this hard. Didn't need me. No doubt about it when this is over I'll miss the food.

Share with Curt the saga of Pi's origins Jordan had delivered to fill the silence.

"Up to taking a look at some charts?"

"Sure."

"Follow me. Bring your beer and trash."

Moved the bookcase aside. Opened the door to inner sanctum and flip the light.

Curt walks straight to the blackboard and starts reading as I close the door. Hears the bookcase roll back in place.

"Clever, bookcase hides the entrance when you're working. It's like a cave. Who rigged this set up?"

"Clayton helped when Maddy rented me this end of the warehouse. Took us most of a year to put it together. You know there were some heavy guys after my hide when I came back from California. Still out there as far as I know."

"I haven't seen one of these since we were kids. They're green now. Seems silly, but I still call them blackboards. Any other way out?"

"Always have a bolt hole. It's a stair."

I show him the hidden pull down leading to my garage area. Standing on the remains of the rusted mesh flooring I point to the iron crossbeams high above the stone floor.

"Night Rusty saved my bacon, crawled in the dark from Sam's side across those with Yippi zipped in his jacket. Managed to climb down and hid in the bed of my truck. Could have broken his damn fool neck."

"My God, Evan! Standing up here makes me seasick. How do you get down? How far to the floor?"

"Iron ladder on the wall behind the debris. Fifty feet. Where they stacked the barrels to age. Slings, on pulleys, put them in place on timbers made out of peeled and squared up trees. The ones not eaten up by termites, wood bees, and wasps became the inside walls of the shelter and my place.

Packed the spaces with insulation to make living space easier to heat. Used horsefeathers to seal the joints."

"Horsefeathers?"

"Long strips of wood ripped from a log with a drawing knife."

"I thought it was Colonel Potter's coined swear word to get past the censors on M*A*S*H*.

Chapter 29

Curt digs through my notes. Keeps looking at the board.

"Don't put up the stuff you told me about the home."

"Why?"

"Clouds the issue."

"It may clear a motive?"

"How?"

"Evan, look at your arrows. Where do they lead?"

"Petra."

"Miss McIntyre. Passed off as child of the Dialmans. Both murdered. Adopted by Marcus McIntyre who was murdered shortly after Clara Dialman. She lived in that hell hole – was moved. Quiet for sixteen years. Maybe the guy thought she was one of those the kids described as 'never came back' or never learned she existed."

"She returns as an adult. Dialman is murdered. Florence Emmens, who was matron of children's home when Petra was in residence, murdered. Same gun used in three of the deaths."

"In a nutshell."

"All arrows lead to the girl and to the children's home."

"True, but where does it get us? Clayton said she suffers from psychological amnesia. I saw it happen the night Clayton was shot. Next day, didn't know he'd been in the house.

"I've questioned her. Unless she's lying she doesn't remember much about her early childhood."

"The killer doesn't know she doesn't."

"Same conclusion Clayton reached. Reason he hired me to look after her. Believes she saw McIntyre's killer."

"I have an suspicion she was aware of the goings on at the home. Thought about hypnosis?"

"Scares the hell out of me. In the hospital some yea-who doctor used it on a kid suffering from battle fatigue. Went off his rocker. Permanent resident in a looney bin.

"This afternoon she started into a glassy stare. Jordan brought her back."

Pi's tough. Not tough enough.

"All right, just a suggestion. Let's sleep on it and take a fresh look in the morning."

~ ~ ~

Curt heads for the bunk house. Close up shop after taking another long look at the board.

Don't know what woke me. Wide awake. Mind churning. Clock reads eleven. Fix a pot of coffee. Go back to work.

Study the board. Check it against my notes.

When this case's over, to play it safe I'll destroy to fine ash, notes, used typewriter ribbons, tapes, and carbon paper. Take the ashes for a long ride on the lake.

Maddy gets more than half of her information from waste baskets beside desks.

Missing something.

Dreaming when I wake up. Idea hangs in the back of my mind.

Look at the board one last time. Can't pry it loose.

Go back to apartment. Freshen up coffee. Wander outside.

Effort to breathe. Air hangs heavy and sultry. Sign of an approaching storm.

Walk down. Study the old river as it chugs past my feet. Long journey to reach the Ohio, then the Mississippi where it spills into the Gulf. Picking up garbage, dropping trash. Over and over, endlessly repeating the cycle.

Case's the same. Questions with no answers. Victims span a quarter of a century. Does it take as long for a single drop of water to travel down the river?

Wander back up to the old spool. Benches worn smooth where we've parked our butts night after night watching water move down stream. Don't have the heart to sit and contemplate. Go back inside to drop into my recliner.

Begin to review each person dead or alive as people. TT only one I can interview. Last session didn't end on good terms.

When I get to Marcus McIntyre, mind pulls over and parks. What do I know about him?

Clayton told me he was a cousin to Mary Laurence. He and her aunt, Ophelia had some kind of hush-hush rescue mission going for years. Kept notes on crimes against children. Married to Jordan's mother. Adopted Petra whose supposed parents live across the street.

Street – McIntyre lived in the same house on Clay Avenue his entire life. Dialman same. Both houses ransacked. What in the hell is the son-of-a-bitch searching for?

Top notch lawyer. McIntyre had a small fortune in his pocket. Didn't take the jewelry? Money isn't the issue.

McIntyre wrote Ophelia Laurence a letter, promising to continue searching for a pedophile, rumored to be operating in Capital City. Dated in May, a few weeks before Clara Dialman was murdered in June.

Curt's right. Killings center around the home and its activities of exploitation of children. McIntyre mentioned the place in his dying breaths.

God damn brain, where have you been? He wasn't trying to give Clayton instructions as to secure shelter for Pi. He was struggling to expose the exploitation of children at the home. Clayton made a grave error. He didn't understand what McIntyre was trying to tell him. Didn't know enough about the situation to draw the right conclusion.

Must talk to Clayton. Nearly midnight. Eleven in Allerton County. Not too late. Dial. Knew McIntyre.

Discuss McIntyre's covert activities. He adds a few details which aren't important. Tell him about Curt's day at the home. He explodes.

"Holly Hell! Glad Mary didn't stumble on the mess when she was holding the fort after her aunt died. She'd of been up there with blades burning."

"Clayton, we're at a wall. Think back. Did McIntyre say anything else?"

"He was on his way out. He struggled to tell me something, but cashed his chips in the middle of the word 'about'."

"Thanks. Tell Mary, hello."

"I will when she gets back from shopping for baby clothes. Gone to Tennessee to some outlets near Crossville with Connie Ames and Maud Tosh."

Talk with Clayton added to the muddle.

Last word, "about." What had McIntyre wanted to tell him?

Stare at the board until it's spinning around TT in circles. Names, places, and events leading to elimination of witnesses.

Witnesses to what?

Told him I didn't do murder. It's for experts. I'm an evidence collector, not an evaluator. Couldn't see the facts for the events until Curt slammed them in my face.

Read across the names. Stop. Read again. Left out two.

Don't know the man's name so I write gardener. Fished out of a pond a week after Pi left. Clayton said he'd been in a fight.

Like hell he had – he'd been beaten. Draw lines to Clara and Robert Dialman.

Wild guessing. Someone figured out the connection between the gardener and Pi. Didn't know the manner of the gardener, a crippled spook, same as he underestimated the determination of Clara Dialman to protect her daughter.

How much did Robert Dialman know? The day his wife was murdered he was out-of-town, until a half-hour before he met TT at the banquet hall.

What in the hell happened in June, 1964, to precipitated sixteen years of murders, putting Pi's life in jeopardy?

Last notation up is TT's shadow. He's so unimportant even Curt didn't catch my omission.

Write Abbott on the end of the board. What do I know about him?

Married to TT's niece for twenty years. Covers up her dependence on the bottle. Content to drift through an easy life running errands. Doesn't he have any ambition other than playing second banana to an aging politician?

Of course, he has. Any man who is half a man does. Filed suit to block Pi's inheritance of the Dialman estate. Didn't pan out. Does he have any money other than what TT dribbles out?

Always around, but isn't involved. Invisible as a shadow on a dark night. Evening Clara Dialman died he didn't attend the dinner. Wife was in the hospital.

Curt said TT delegated the supervision of the children's home to him. Denied any knowledge of wrong doing. Downy kid ran up to him. Scared him when he started rubbing him and yelling.

Terrified him.

I'm a fucking stupid moron.

Heard what I wanted to hear. Not what was said.

Kid terrified him. Kid knew the score. Fingered him. Would have killed the kid if the yard hadn't been full of witnesses.

McIntyre's last word wasn't "about."

It was Abbott!

Chapter 30

Turn chair over getting out. Slam bookcase in place. Dial Pi as I scramble into whatever I can lay my hands to.

Operator's flat voice informs me the number dialed's out of order. Do I wish to file a report?

Grab my keys and run to the shelter.

Shake Curt awake.

"Abbott. Call Billy Ray. Going to McIntyre's."

Come near stripping reverse out of the Charger's gear box as I gun it out of the garage. Skid around the warehouse throwing gravel to the road.

Ignore every speed limit racing to the alley. Backend kites as it slides to the gate.

It's ajar. Nudge it open. Drive to back door.

Run to side of the house. Phone line cut.

Back door locked.

Break window. Reach in cutting my arm. Sprint through laundry room.

Where is Whoof? Should be barking his head off.

Round the corner under the stairs as Pi comes rolling down in a tight ball.

Abbott behind her trying to kick her in the head.

She lands in a gymnastic tumble. Springs to her feet in a flash.

Grabs a walking stick from tall jar.

Spins on the balls of her feet. Screaming an ungodly screech.

"Pi, get out of the way. Run."

She doesn't hear me. Blocking me.

Can't get to him. She's in the way.

Stick has a knob like a club.

She takes a wild swing at Abbott. Misses taking out the ball on the end of the stair rail.

Abbott pulls a gun from his pocket.

"You damn nigger. I'll kill you."

She pulls her left hand up over her heart. Left leg back – right forward.

Stick doesn't pause as she spins to his side.

Going into the gun.

Stick descends straight down with all the force in her body.

Knob strikes Abbott's wrist, sending the gun flying into the jar. Shatters on impact.

Abbott's fighting for the stick with his left hand. Right, dangles out of commission.

Brat screams, "Bad man threw me down the stairs."

Voice isn't hers. High pitched like a child's.

She drops to a crouch.

Lightening fast, the point of the stick drives up for Abbott's throat as she rises from the floor.

"Bad man put mummy in the trunk. She never came back."

Springs back like a dancer out of his reach. Stabbing blow after blow with the stick into his chest.

Doesn't stop moving.

She keeps between me and Abbott.

Reach for my gun. It isn't there!

Back at the warehouse.

"I'd lend you mine, but you might hit her."

Curt's voice at my shoulder shakes what sense I have out of me.

Bite my lip to keep from yelling. Not a damn thing we can do with Pi in our way slashing like a whirling dervish striking at Abbott.

He lunges toward her. Gets hold of the stick.

She whirls away dragging him off his feet.

Takes the stick in both hands near the ends.

Brings it up in a snapping move that meets his chin as he falls.

Springs like a wild cat on a weasel.

Her knees land on the shattered wrist.

Stick smashes down with savage force above his elbow.

Abbott screams. His left hand beating the floor in agony.

Pi looks up. Sees us. Yells.

"Hey Rubes. Need some help."

Whoof plunges through the glass of the storm door.

Knocks her sprawling. Clamps a choke hold on Abbott's throat.

"Time we broke it up. We can't let Whoof kill him."

"Why not?"

Two steps get me to the carnage.

"Whoof, release. He's mine."

He obeys my command.

Curt helps Pi to her feet. Tears are streaming down her face.

"He killed my mother! I saw him!"

Grab Abbott up by his shirt front. Blood's seeping from his neck where Whoof had set to kill.

Hold him up with my left hand.

Deliver openhanded and backhanded blows with the other.

One for every life he destroyed.

Lose count.

Keep slapping him until Billy Ray steps through the shattered storm door as the storm breaks.

Cruiser's lights flashing through the rain out front.

Give Abbott a hard shove.

"Cuff him.

"Book him.

"Tried to kill her!

"Gun in the mess."

Pull Pi to me. She's shaking like a leaf in a high wind. A jacket's hanging on the hall tree.

Reach for it to put around her. Touch two clubs connected by a thick chain. A pair of nunchukus!

Take it off the hook, raise the lid of the seat of hall tree. Drop it in as I drape the jacket around her shoulders.

Sit on the seat and pull her into my lap. Don't need her found with an Oriental weapon of destruction. Take too damn long to explain what it is. Pray her gun's upstairs.

She curls into me like a lost kitten. Same as the night I found her. Has a case of hiccups or giggles.

Watch the fun. Curt's sidearm's fastened over green sweats too short for his arms or legs. Keeping us out of it as much as possible. Has a few moments to brief Billy Ray before the press invades.

Promises to let Martin Stokes in on the entire story when I tell him what it is.

Contributes the property damage to Whoof, who's busy shaking bits of shattered glass from his fur. Satisfied he has shed the fragments, plops down in front of us to clean his paws. Picture of innocence.

Pawns the newspaper guy, who followed Billy Ray off on him with a brief comment to the effect he's exhausted from a brutal day. Lets him take the credit for the collar as Johnson was struggling with Abbott when the guy entered.

Pi wiggles and sits up surveying the damage to her hall as two patrolmen frog march Abbott out to a cruiser.

"Are you okay?"

"Buy a new horse. The cavalry was slow."

Chapter 31

Johnson got rid of the reporters by telling them the chief would hold a news conference, to explain the details of what had been an ongoing investigation by the department in the morning.

Double speak for I don't know anymore than you do, from a seasoned investigator.

Thankfully, the local boys buy it. Pi isn't in any kind of shape to be interviewed.

How do you tell guys from the fourth estate: two grown men stood helpless while a small girl used a walking stick to subdued a deranged killer in no time flat?

We look at each other in a dazed manner. Soldiers, who've survived a long exhausting battle. Hard to believe we came though with so few scratches.

Brat declares she's starving.

Look at my watch. One thirty. Longest two and a half hours I've ever endured, outside a nightmare.

"Bihn's open for a half hour."

"Call him. Tell him we're on our way while I get dressed."

She's barefoot with glass all over the hall, wearing those poka-dotted pajamas and a jacket spotted with blood.

Pick her up and set her on a step away from the glass. She darts up the stairs with Whoof on her heels.

Curt picks up the ball finial from the floor. Attempts to set it right. Moves it back and forth. Takes it off and reaches into the column. Pulls out a pale pink envelope. Holds it up to the light. Turns it over.

"This is addressed to Miss McIntyre. No return address."

"Give it to me. I'll see she gets it."

"It may be evidence. What he was searching for."

"Maybe, but it's addressed to her. Hand it over."

"You know they aren't going to believe us."

"Why do you think I agreed to this after midnight supper? Need to coordinate the lies."

Desper and Charity pick their way though the glass, wearing their robes, shaking a golf umbrella.

"Go get dressed. It's over. Join us.

"We're going to Bihn's. I intend to tell this heinous story one time, then I'm out. Taking an extended vacation."

Asked, Pat to fix a big platter of fried chicken with all the fixings.

He'd had a busy night. He retorts he'd order-in, from the Colonel's. Blessings of living in a university town. They're open all night for students who don't have enough sense to go to bed.

Suggest he use his best judgement for six or make it seven, if he wants to have a front row seat to the nastiest story of the century.

Pat hustles us into the Blue Room. No windows. Takes drink orders. Raises an eyebrow when we order coffee or iced tea. Table's set for seven. He isn't about to miss our conversation.

Billy Ray helps him carry food from the kitchen. He'd piled the take-outs into large bowls. Serves it family style. No one says a word as we tackle the offerings.

Curt winks at me. It's all we can do to keep from laughing. We'd consumed a large meal a few hours earlier, yet we are as hungry as those who hadn't eaten supper.

"What am I going to tell the chief? We have a prominent citizen in lockdown. Charges cover half a page. Man is raving. Every stoolie Towbridge has in the department is keeping the lines hot.

"Duncan Abbott looks like he's been worked over with a billy club not counting a deep animal bite near his larynx and a smashed wrist.

"Blade, I've never seen a man hand-whipped."

"Captain wouldn't let Whoof kill him."

"You destroyed him."

Dog perks up. Stares at Pat, who slips him a biscuit stuffed with a chicken breast. Scoots out his chair. Turns it around and straddles it. Leans on the back, sipping a beer.

"Start your report: Capital City Police Department, in conjunction with the State Police completed an intensive investigation with the apprehension of Duncan Abbott blab…blab. You know the drill.

"Use longest possible words to spill the least possible information."

"Where did you learn to write reports?"

"Curt, ever read an insurance policy?"

"Don't know anyone who does."

"I do. Sometimes for both sides, depends on who's paying for my time. Part of the job.

"Client's entitled to a final report for every case I take. Unlike lawyers, if a problem ends up in court, my records can be subpoenaed as evidence."

Billy Ray's scratching his head.

"What led you to suspect Abbott for the murders?"

"Curt's yesterday will be in the morning paper. He told me a few items that won't make print. It's a family paper… gory details are suppressed.

"Called Clayton Forrester. He discovered McIntyre's body. Man was able to say a few words before he died. He tried to tell Forrester about something with his last breath.

"Sitting in the dark, tossing information around when little pieces fell into place, to jive with old departmental reports and newspaper clippings. McIntyre named his killer...Abbott."

We go over all the monstrous details. Billy Ray and Curt eliminating items. Forgotten on purpose are Curt's rookies and their work on Fog Landing, which's pending. Didn't want to speculate how many kids from the home exited down a ready made sewer.

Brat sits through it with eyes wide and mouth stuffed with chicken. Looks as if a couple died on her plate.

"Hate to go home. I know a reporter or the chief is waiting for my hide. Feel like I'm on the lam."

"No need. Maddy Sorals has a hideout for fugitives with all the comforts of home. I'm using her accommodations tonight. You can join me. Noon tomorrow sounds like a better time to make the scene.

"Call your wife and tell her to pack a change of clothes for you in a garbage bag. Set it out on the street. Evan will pick it up while I escort Miss McIntyre home..."

Start to protest. He holds up his hand.

"If anyone is hanging around her place it will look like she's been in my office making an official statement. Desper, you and Charity go with me."

"Slick how the new Captain made off with your girl."

"Pat, she's a client. He's a master at strategy. Served under him in 'Nam. Got home in one piece following his orders."

"Never figured Abbott did anything except pickup after Towbridge."

"You don't know the half of it. Don't want to know. If I were you I'd scrub out the place with Lysol to rid it of his stink."

~ ~ ~

Next morning I deliver her letter. She reads it. Hands it back to me. Runs to the bathroom.

As I suspected it was written by Clara Dialman. A loving letter to a beloved daughter she'd given away to protect her from a dangerous predator. Letter was meant for her when she was grown and could appreciate the sacrifice her mother had to make to keep her safe.

Clara Dialman walked in on Abbott forcing his penis into the mouth of her small daughter. Vivian had bitten him. He'd had the audacity to call his penis 'nature's pacifier.' She'd taken her daughter across the street to Marcus McIntyre, begging him to protect her from harm while she dealt with Abbott.

Dialman was out of town and not expected to return until just before the dinner.

The letter's from a distraught woman who was obligated to make a public appearance she could not avoid. Writing from her heart in disjointed words and phrases, working in a frenzy to get the entire story down on paper and into safe hands. It's obvious she was aware her life was in grave danger.

I imagine, during the long beating she sustained before she died, she taunted him with the letter's existence. Clara Dialman had a special kind of stubborn courage.

"Brat, I'm sorry. I wouldn't have given it to you…"

"Evan, I'm grown up. Don't try to protect me. Yes, it made me sick to see in my mother's words, what he was trying to do to me."

"What do you want me to do with it?"

"Give it to Uncle T. He must see it. Tell him to destroy it. I sure as hell don't want it turning up in a court room as evidence."

"Will do. About last night…"

"You learned what I've been tying to tell you. I know how to protect myself. I learned from Juan Torres. I told you he taught me to shoot. He has a fishing boat on the bay."

"The nunchukus?"

"A graduation present. Juan is from the Phillippines who came here during WWII. Watched his family assassinated by the Japanese. He took them off a solider he killed."

"I see."

I do more than she does. Juan Torres 's one of Clayton Forrester's hand picked spies. Sent to guard his ward.

"The term…"

She giggles.

"I didn't know it was Whoof's signal to attack."

"How?"

"Clayton took me to a carnival on a farm below the academy where I went to high school. There was a fight and one guy yelled it. Got all the workers running to help.

"He knew Mr. Moss, who owned the farm. Arranged for me to take riding lessons."

"It's a carney reference. Call for help. When Marc Puckett trained Whoof I thought it was one he wouldn't hear by accident."

"Billy Bejaysus. Don't be so glum. It worked."

Chapter 32

Brat's throwing a party. Bihn let her have the Blue room for her wing-ding.

Busy creating her world. Nuts over her half-sister. Rusty's giving her lessons in the proper way to hold a baby. He gained his vast experience with Welding Forge.

I'll say this for her, even if she keeps the name McIntyre gave her, she has given her whole heart to tiny, Leesa Morgan.

Their mutual love of salt water and sailing sealed a relationship between father and daughter which includes Jordan Ames. There's a universal kinship among those who ply the oceans. She plans to visit Seamew Island in the fall, after the tourists have abandoned the beaches.

Sargent Billy Ray Johnson and his new sidekick, Patrolman Desper Sims with their wives are in attendance. Brat is excited about the promotion and new hire, as this makes Desper the first Negro police officer on the city force.

Maddy dropped by earlier to pay her respects. Didn't stay. Won't accept condolences. She looks drawn as if she's not sleeping. Sam's death was hard to take. When she discovered who sold her out, it was the crowning blow.

No desire to know the details. Woman hasn't been seen for weeks. If she's dead that's one body they'll never find.

We're holding up a back wall sipping Falls Cities.

Out of a job.

Jordan's on hold till the formalities of Dialman's estate are completed. Curt's hard to live with since he made captain.

"The story in the morning paper made interesting reading. TT Towbridge resigning the lieutenant governorship due to family health problems."

"True. Faith Abbott's in a private clinic. Got her sobered enough to talk. Her uncle's adamant she will be unavailable to testify in court. Curt got her story."

"Abbott threw his wife down the stairs the afternoon before TT's sister was murdered. Clara Dialman told Faith about her husband. She confronted him. Been drowning sixteen years of living in terror with booze."

"Look who's here."

"Managed to haul in the former second stringer. Quite a coup."

"No surprise. Pat told me TT reserved a table out front for two o'clock every weekday afternoon. Paper neglected to mention he didn't resign as head of the party. Sis is a frequent guest. Towbridge introduces her as his niece."

"Yeah. Takes her to church and then to Rolling Acres County Club for Sunday dinner."

"He recognizes she is both brilliant and shrewd. Never had to explain a thing, but once. She had it down pat. Uses it with interesting twists of her own.

"They worked a deal. She is ceding him his lifetime interest in her part of the Towbridge family estate with interesting strings as to progeny and the children's home. She is going to act as his hostess."

"To what?"

"Official and private occasions."

"Didn't miss a beat getting Pi in his stable."

"Evan, you're cynical."

"Hint of the tar brush doesn't bother him?"

"Give the devil his due. Never a question. Family didn't own slaves – may have been active in the Underground Railroad. One kept John Hunt Morgan out of Capital City and away from the locks and railroad."

For a guy who lived away for years, he comes out with little tidbits of information I've never heard.

Free labor supply in the name of goodness and light. Used children. Didn't need slaves.

TT has a motive for everything he does. Wouldn't know how to operate any other way. In time he'll find a way to capitalize on her heritage.

Desperate for a visible hostess. Faith Abbott's in no

shape to handle the pressure of parties with gallons of booze within reach.

"He sees her as the little girl he took to the movies and bought a stuffed elephant. Has a reverence for the fancy college she attended back east. Wait till he runs afoul of her finishing school education on the docks of Chesapeake Bay. Has a vocabulary salty enough to make a longshoreman blush."

Ames lets Pi lead him around by the nose. Needs an education where she's concerned.

"Shock discovering that despite a network of spies to equal M16 they missed catching the big gar."

"Towbridge is pushing for the death penalty. He won't be satisfied until Abbott is drawn and quartered or literally publicly castrated before the execution. Judge Roach said the District Attorney is still shaking from the explosion."

"Jordan, normal crooks are an odd bunch of ducks. They will commit any type of heinous crime, but molesting children is a cardinal sin. Pedophiles seldom survive long enough to come to trial. In all my years of law enforcement, Duncan Abbott is the first true hardcore pedophile I've ever encountered."

"Abbott destroyed Towbridge's public career. He'll never be able to crawl out from under the fallout."

"Doesn't intend to. Setting up to be the power broker from behind the scenes."

"Took a page out of your book?"

"What?"

"You. You work at night in the shadows."

"No choice with my mug."

"There'll always be a reporter asking questions. Digging for the real scoop. No one believes it. The ugliest scandal of the century and he was entirely innocent."

"I don't. Yet in this case I know it's true."

"Evan, how?"

"Check I cashed at the bank this morning. Way back, he told me he'd triple the amount Forrester paid me to find who killed his sister. Gave him a copy of my final report and Clara Dialman's letter.

"Presented a bill showing Clayton's funding. Did it as a joke, wasn't serious. He wrote the check without batting an eye."

"You're kidding. I saw the money he sent you."

"Only part of it. He'd already given me what was in his billfold and what was in the briefcase. Clayton never travels without being well heeled."

"What are you going to do?"

"Make a healthy contribution to Bobbi's college fund then spend the rest of the summer with my feet up on the rail watching Harbor Master work."

"TT is leaving."

"Capital City is like all small towns. He's a crook. We know it, but he is our crook."

"Thank you for your words of wisdom. Time to take the 'hostess' home. Whoof's getting fat. Come to think of it, so's Yippi."

Lady of the hour's drunk. Can't hold more than one beer. Rusty been sneaking sips. Curt's responsibility. Brat's mine.

"Before you go. Abbott is singing. Bragging is a sickening, but better word. Odd thing is, he hasn't named anyone else. May not know the Emmens woman had other unidentified customers, but those boys got names from somewhere. Been telling us how clever he was getting Whoof out of the action.

"He broke into your locker at the gym and emptied it of your dirty clothes. Dragged them down the alley to the stable where you park and threw them in a dark corner. Went back to Petra's and opened the back gate. When she let Whoof out he followed your scent to the stable. Abbott locked him in. Back of the stable is shattered.

"Going to get her a dog of her own. Easier on buildings and furnishings."

"One more thing."

"What?"

"Took a call from a lady for you."

"Who?"

"Sheba Cross, remember her?"

Oh God, I'd been so busy with this case I hadn't taken time to give her a buzz. I recognize the emphasis Curt puts on 'lady.' Sheba runs a good show.

Truth Blade. She never crossed your mind.

"Her message was she got bored waiting. She got married to Horace Langbourne. Number no longer in service."

The name rings a bell. Horses, long face looks like one. H. T. Langbourne has interests in stakes racing. Good for her. She deserves more than I have to offer, even if her best friends would never think of her as a lady.

"Thanks. Meet me for breakfast.

"Party's over. Cinderella's soused. Guest's can't leave until she does."

Leave 'em to chew the fat.

It's over for me.

Running, sure. Be a spell before I can sit at the spool table and not think of Sam. He was a friend. Too many friends washed away by the sands of time.

"My job is finished. Promised Connie a delayed honeymoon.

"I will be back for the finals, which are nothing more than formalities. Keep an eye on him."

"He has got it bad."

"I noticed. Pi worships him."

"He is too old for her."

"Not Sis. She is too old for him. Should be the battle of the Titans when they wake-up."

"Star-crossed lovers are out of my jurisdiction."

~ ~ ~

"Why are you leaving town?"

"Give dog a break. Whoof's gaining weight going to Bihn's with you. Needs to chase rabbits and squirrels. Run off some of the flab."

"I wasn't talking about your dog."

"Same goes here. Unless you've forgotten, I have a foster daughter who deserves attention."

"Bobbi?"

"Yes. Nine years old. Lost both of her parents. Good kid."

"Rusty told me about her."

"Anvil and Doris take good care of her when I'm not around. Worked out for all parties. They've a baby now. She's my responsibility."

"I suppose so."

"Don't pull a down in the dumps. You'll be busy."

"I was counting on you being around to show us some of the ropes."

"Us?"

"Mary Forrester. As soon as the baby comes and Clayton is out of the woods, she is going back to work."

"Yes, she and Connie Ames have a tax and secretarial business in Clydesville. What do they have to do with you?"

Brat keeps twisting a curl around her finger. Looking like a lost puppy.

"She is going to reopen her pipeline for at-risk children."

"Clayton's okay with the idea?"

"He is her husband, not her keeper. She accepts it when he disappears, sometimes gone for as long as a year. He must abide by her interests."

Like hell he will. Brat has no idea the gardener was one of his men, who'd taken a bullet in the hip and was unable to work in the field. The favor he did Clayton cost him his life.

George Stanopolis and Juan Torres are two more he placed in strategic positions. Their day jobs are spies who police the docks of the bay for illegal infiltrators. Neither has a qualm of silently eliminating a problem.

"Didn't answer my question. What does this have to do with you?"

"Charity and I talked to Uncle T. We're thinking about reopening the children's home as a memorial to Clara Dialman. It will be closely supervised with only carefully selected employees. A shelter like Sam Sorals', except for children. Maddy is going to help us."

"Where're you going to find the money required to feed and clothe the kids?"

"We've tossed a few ideas back and forth, nothing is settled. Some we could get from Children's Services. They're always short of emergency shelters. We don't want long term residents."

"Why?"

"Evan, Charity lived in a Catholic home her entire life until she married Desper. I lived in one for seven years. Something happens. It doesn't work, even in the best places. I can't explain it."

"Becomes a training ground for cons."

"That's cynical."

"No, it's the truth. Knew them on the circuit.

"Brat, rethink your schemes. Where Towbridge's concerned keep your money in your shoe. Your check book locked in a safe."

"You don't like Uncle T?"

"Sure as hell don't trust him."

"You work for him."

"Pi, work I do for him barely keeps Whoof in dog food."

"He admires you."

"Refuse to be his lackey.

"Back up. What did you mean by 'showing you the ropes'?"

"I'm going to open a detective agency."

"You're going to do…what?"

I'd love to shake her till her teeth rattle.

"You heard me. I'm opening a detective agency."

"Have you lost what few marbles you ever had?"

"My marbles are fine, thank you. I have a degree in criminology from Maryland."

"How does it apply to Kentucky?"

"Captain Colton said I had all the credentials to take the State Police exam."

"Being polite to an idiot. You'd flunk the physical before you got through the door."

"I'm in good shape."

"No question. Take their recruits from 5'9 to 6'2. Require an even row when they line up wearing their Smokey the Bear hats. What are you 4'10?"

"I can take care of myself."

"You showed us. Hasn't it taught you anything?"

"What do you mean?"

"Damn it, Brat. PI work's ninety-five percent drudgery. Digging in files…records…people's lives. Sitting in a parked car at night following someone around. What happens if you have to go to the john?"

"Find a gas station."

"You've taken your eye off the subject. While you hit the bushes, he takes off. Wasted client's money. If you're spotted you can get your head blown off. Wandering husbands don't take kindly to being followed."

"Uncle T thinks I'd be a natural."

"I'll bet he does, 's he going to supply clients?"

"When I'm with him I meet people."

"Not much for maintaining a low profile. Who'd be stupid enough to hire a PI whose name and picture keep appearing on the society page?"

"Could be an advantage instead of a liability."

"Not with the company you've been keeping."

"You sound like you're jealous."

"Of who?"

"Uncle T."

Jealous? Idiotic nonsense. Brat twists everything I say.

"Of all the dumb statements you've made, that one takes the brass ring."

"You're the most arrogant piece of low life I've ever had the displeasure to be associated."

"You're a mark asking to be skinned."

"Go back to your hole. See if I care."

"Planning to. Time's wasted here. I won't be here to bail you out."

"Bail me out! Who ended up in a hospital?"

"Point taken. Dangerous to be around you."

Brat's cute when she's spitting nails. Eyes glitter like she's stalking a mouse. Her bottom lip sticks out in a pout. A kissable lip.

"Get this through your thick skull. I am opening a detective agency."

"Suit yourself. What are you going call it, Petticoats for Hire?"

"You are being insulting and insinuating."

"Intended to since you won't listen to reason. Keep evading my questions."

"If you ever used the front entrance you'd know. My name is beside the door."

"Seen it. Any woman with a grain of sense uses her initials, even in the phone book. You had Desper put it there for the mailman."

"Did not. It was there when I arrived. Desper said it has been there since they started working for Clayton."

"Don't come crying to me when you get yourself killed."

Lobster Cantonese

Evan Blade orders Lobster Cantonese from Bihn's and declares it Ambrosia. See if you agree. Our long time family favorite for Thanksgiving or Christmas. My sister once called me for the recipe. When we arrived, she'd neglected to tell us we had to cook it since she bought the ingredients. Dinner was late.

6 (8oz) thawed rock lobster tails
olive oil
minced garlic to taste
½ pound of pork loin, cubed
2 T. cornstarch

¼ cup soy sauce
2 carrots - sliced
½ t. black pepper
2 cups boiling water
½ cup slivered green onions

1. Cut white membrane of lobster. Remove from shell in single piece. Slice crosswise into inch sections.

2. Precook carrot pennies in the microwave.

3. Heat oil in large skillet. Add garlic and pork, saute, stirring until pork is no longer pink. 10 minutes or so.

4. In a small bowl, make a smooth paste of cornstarch and 1/3 cup of water.

5. Stir into pork the cooked carrots, soy sauce, pepper, boiling water, and cornstarch mixture. Bring to a firm

boil. Reduce heat and simmer, stirring until thickened and translucent – again about 10 minutes.

6. Add lobster pieces; cook over very low heat until lobster is tender or turns opaque. Do not over cook.

7. Serve over a bed of wild rice mixture. We use Royal Blend – Rice Select. Add green onions as garnish. Serve piping hot.

Serves six. Easy to double or triple. Total prep time from start to finish about one hour.

Green salad and dinner rolls will have your family and guests begging to be invited next year.

Delegate someone else for dessert.

Acknowledgments

No novel is written without the help of many people, who dig out little tidbits of information or provide you with the directions to work the Internet, to discover it for yourself.

We want to thank Rose Baker, who used her skills as a former legal assistant to uncover the intricacies of Kentucky Statues, of the time period which pertained to our story.

Thanks goes to Patrick Bihn, a life long personal friend who allowed us to use his name, as the owner of a fine bar and grill. Hope you enjoy your new persona, Pat.

Many thanks goes to Marc Puckett, a former student and master sergeant, retired from the United States Army who filled us in on dog training.

Barbara Morgan spent many hours culling a rough manuscript for mistakes. Without her help we would have been lost.

Praises to Paula Nason, who used her skills to help us polish the final edition of *Forged Blade* for full publication. Her help and friendship are deeply appreciated.

A deep thank you goes to Mr. Paul Cundiff, owner of *Woodies Restorations*, in Russell Springs, KY, who took the time to provide information on the restoration of antique wooden boats and the engines that powered them. He provided us with the information that the same engine was used in both Greyhound buses and Fairlane cabin cruisers.

A second heads up goes to Mr. James Osborne, the manager of *Woodies Restorations,* who located a picture of a Detroit 6-71 TIB Marine Diesel Engine for us on the Internet so we could describe it in a future novel.

A very special thank you goes to Stuart Simpson, who used vague suggestions and photographs, taken in different lighting conditions, to combine them to create the cover for the Evan Blade series.

We thank Barbara Appleby and Jerry Sampson, who studied our cover mockups and provided us with valuable suggestions as to the use of visual elements.

A big thanks to those who hang out on the Facebook group page, *Lake Cumberland Boaters*, who jogged my memory with notes that a Fairlane cabin cruiser was used in the TV series, *Gilligan's Island.*

Kudos go to the librarians, who man the telephones at The Kentucky Department of Libraries and Archives, who exercised extended patience in answering many questions about locations of buildings in Frankfort, KY, that were demolished before they were born.

About the Author

Nash Black is the husband and wife team of Ford Nashett and Irene Black. The couple write ghost, mystery and detective stories based in fictional Ono County, KY where murder and mayhem are a way of life. When not writing they enjoy live theater, boating, auto racing, fishing, and photography.

A special honor for Irene and Ford was the Nash Black Photography Award presented on Earth Day for the best photographs submitted to an annual contest. The award was named for them using their pen name by the Fruit of the Lens Camera Club, located at Somerset Community College in Somerset, KY.

They are storytellers, whose purpose is to entertain. Traditional mysteries, detective stories, and ghost stories are their stage and microphone. In particular, their ghost stories are written to be read aloud or told to audiences of all ages without bringing small children to screams and tears.

They write for the people who spend time waiting in a doctor's office, waiting behind the counter in an all-night diner, or drifting along in a skiff hoping the fish will bite.

The settings for their works are small towns and rural areas of Kentucky, encompassed by five major rivers the Cumberland, Tennessee, Ohio, Kentucky, and Mississippi.

Ono is a real hamlet on the shore of Lake Cumberland located in Kentucky, which they used as the fictional name of their imaginary world.

Ono Almanac articles are published each week in local newspapers and a blog (http://onoalmanac.blogspot.com) to illustrate customs and evoke memories of times past with snips and snaps of bit and pieces of Ono County.

Ono Chronicle (http://onochronicle.blogspot.com) is a blog in newspaper style that records the events and lives of the characters in their stories. Previous encounters with the Internal Revenue Service auditors led to their award finalist and highly reviewed Writing as a Small Business, an in-depth study of writing expenses and income authors receive with citations as to the sources.

You can contact them at nashblack.com or onocounty.com.